10·20

ARCADE

AND THE DAZZLING TRUTH DETECTOR

Books by Rashad Jennings

The IF in Life

ARCADE

AND THE **DAZZLING TRUTH DETECTOR**

RASHAD JENNINGS

WITH JILL OSBORNE

ZONDERKIDZ

Arcade and the Dazzling Truth Detector
Copyright © 2020 by Rashad Jennings, LLC
Illustrations © 2020 by Rashad Jennings

Requests for information should be addressed to:
Zonderkidz, *3900 Sparks Dr. SE, Grand Rapids, Michigan 49546*

Library of Congress Cataloging-in-Publication Data

Names: Jennings, Rashad, 1985-author. | Osborne, Jill, 1961-author.
Title: Arcade and the dazzling truth detector / Rashad Jennings; with Jill Osborne.
Description: Grand Rapids, Michigan: Zonderkidz, 2020. | Series: The coin slot chronicles; 4 |
    Audience: Ages 8 & Up. | Summary: The Triple T Token takes Arcade and Zoe Livingston
    to the highest, lowest, deepest, coldest, and hottest places on Earth and to some of the
    greatest moments in history, leading them on a whirlwind journey to discover themselves
    and the secrets of the Triple T Token.
Identifiers: LCCN 2020013503 (print) | LCCN 2020013504 (ebook) | ISBN 9780310767442
    (hardcover) | ISBN 9780310767497 (epub)
Subjects: CYAC: Adventure and adventurers—Fiction. | Brothers and
sisters—Fiction. | Voyages and travels—Fiction. | Magic—Fiction. |
African Americans—Fiction.
Classification: LCC PZ7.1.J4544 Al 2020 (print) | LCC PZ7.1.J4544 (ebook)
| DDC [Fic]—dc23
LC record available at https://lccn.loc.gov/2020013503
LC ebook record available at https://lccn.loc.gov/2020013504

Illustrated by: Alan Brown

Art direction: Cindy Davis
Interior design: Denise Froehlich

Printed in the United States of America

20 21 22 23 24 25 26 27 28 29 /LSC/ 10 9 8 7 6 5 4 3 2 1

This book is dedicated to my dad—the late
ALBERT O. JENNINGS.

My dad, the patriarch of my family, Albert Jennings, has gone home to be with the Lord. Though I know I'll see him again, I'll miss his laughter. We became so close that whenever he was very tired, and Mom needed to get his attention, she'd just mention my name and he'd light right up! Yet despite the wonderfully close relationship he and I had, there will always be one thing I'll remember most. You see, Dad was a man's man with a gruff exterior. He was never a hand-holder. But a few days before his passing, when I was last at his bedside, we hugged and shook hands as always. But that last time, he literally took my hand and held it tightly for five minutes! In that moment, I made special promises to him that I will forever keep. It was like he knew it would be our last time together in this life. Dad went to heaven at 1:24 am ET, March 1st, which in LA was 10:24 pm PT, February 29th (Leap Day). I'll always remember Leap Day, because throughout his life, my dad made so many courageous leaps for us!

And now, my dad has made one final leap, out of this life
and into the waiting arms of the Lord in heaven. I won't wish
him happy travels—he has arrived! Dad . . . Wish me happy
travels! By God's grace, I'll be there with you, someday!

I love you, Dad, with all my heart.

Prologue

"Theo! Son! Where are you? It is time to get back to work."

Theo Timon Theros sat where he always did during his short afternoon break—on the outside stone window ledge, staring at the mighty Greek arches in the distance, sketching.

"Theo! There you are!" Theo's father huffed and puffed after climbing the steep stairs from the workshop. He raised a hand toward the sky. "How many times can you sketch the same scene?"

Infinity.

Theo had to tear his eyes away from the parchment to answer his father. "Please, may I have a longer break today, since it is my birthday?"

Theo's father, Ergon Theros, the most skilled and, therefore, busiest metalworker in town, grumbled. "Too much rest invites poverty."

"But I'm not resting. I'm . . . imagining possibilities." Theo dropped his head and traced the reed pen over the lines in his drawing.

"Well, then, bring your imagination down to the metal

shop and see if it is possible for you to finish today's project. We will celebrate your birthday this evening. Your mother is helping the servants prepare your favorite dish." Theo's father moved in closer and took Theo's sketch from his hands. He held it up to compare it to the architecture in the distance. "This drawing looks nothing like an arcade. See, you've squared off the arches." Ergon sighed loudly. "This looks more like three Ts joined together."

Theo grinned, gathered his sketching materials, and followed his father downstairs to the workshop. A new, unforged piece of metal sat at his workstation. Theo picked

up the lump, flipping it upside-down and back over, inspecting it.

This is the best we have.

He carefully placed it back on the workbench and faced his father with wide eyes.

"Where is the other piece I was working on?"

Theo's father turned his head slightly toward his son. "Next year you will turn thirteen. What kind of father would I be if I did not bestow a generous gift on the last birthday of your childhood?"

Theo rested both hands on the workbench and stared at the metal. "I do not understand. This is a gift?"

Ergon Theros walked over and placed a hand on Theo's shoulder. "You said you were imagining possibilities. Well, what would you imagine for this little lump of metal? It is yours to shape however you choose. Happy birthday, Theo Timon Theros."

Theo breathed in deeply, his father's hand heavy on his shoulder. This piece of metal represented profit for the family. For his father to give that up was a strong gesture of love from the often serious and frugal man.

"Thank you, Father."

"You are welcome, my son." Theo's father lifted his hand and returned to his projects on the other workbench.

Theo spoke without looking up, his voice cracking slightly. "And when would be a proper time for me to work on it?"

Ergon tipped his head in Theo's direction, and the sides of his mouth pulled up in a grin.

"You may work on it this afternoon only. Quickly now, before the birthday magic fades." He shook his head and took a mallet to his own project.

Theo struggled to swallow the lump that had formed in his throat. His eyes filled up, clouding his vision, but he willed himself not to blink.

He's allowing me to create. But just this one day.

He grabbed his parchment and carefully examined the drawing. The one his father thought was a mis-sketched row of arches.

He took a deep breath . . . gathered the metal and his tools . . . and headed to the heating vat.

Happy birthday, Theo Timon Theros.

He always thought it odd that all his names began with T.

Now I see.

CHAPTER 1

Whack Attack

On January twenty-first, everyone in my life turned weird. Except Doug Baker—my best friend and now foster brother—who normally *is* weird, turned *normal*.

"Dude, I have a list of things I need to pick up at the market. I'll catch you later." Doug and I were walking home from school on our favorite path through Central Park.

"The market? Since when do *you* go to the market?" I adjusted the straps on my flamingo backpack, tightening it on my back. "You know what, seventh grade books are heavy!"

"Hey, Tolleys!" Doug yelled to a couple of big shadows following behind us on the path. "Can Arcade walk home with you guys? I gotta go to the market."

Kevin and Casey Tolley, our "friendly" neighborhood bully brothers, picked up the pace, and when they reached me and Doug, they gave us fist bumps.

Weird!

"Oh, yeah. He can walk with us. We've been wanting to talk with you anyway, Arcade."

"Yeah." The Tolley twin on the left grinned a little,

revealing his chipped tooth. That would be Casey. "We were wondering, Arcade, if you could come to the . . . uh . . . Ivy Park Library with us tomorrow. We wanna start research for our persuasive essays, and you could help us find some good books."

"*You guys* want to go to the library to start a school project *on a Saturday*? You're messin' with me, right?"

I stared at them through my narrowed eyes. These boys *could not be* the real Tolleys. They must have had their bodies snatched by aliens or something.

"We were thinking of goin' at two o'clock," the other one—Kevin—said. "Do you know if the library is open on Saturdays?"

I swung my head around, looking for Doug. But he was outta there.

"Well? What do you say, Arcade?" Casey crossed his arms and stepped back. "I know the project isn't due for a month, but we wanna get a jump on it."

I scanned the Central Park lawn. "You dudes seen a spaceship anywhere?"

"Huh?" Casey and Keven both grunted out.

I shook my head and held back a laugh. "Never mind. Yeeeeeah . . . okay, sure, I'll go. I gotta be back early though. I have plans with the fam."

I didn't know *for sure* if I had plans with my family, but tomorrow was my twelfth birthday. No one had actually mentioned my birthday yet. Mom and Dad had been extra busy with their jobs, and my sister, Zoe, had been swamped with homework. But none of them ever forgot a birthday.

"We appreciate the help, Arcade." Casey walked beside me and pulled a bag of chocolate chip cookies out of a brown bag. "Want one? These are your favorite, right?"

The *only* thing that could make this day *weirder* would be . . .

"Arcade! There you are! How was school?"

It was my sister. She had climbed up the stairs out of the subway station. Her long, black hair was pulled back in a ponytail, as usual.

"ZOE!" I grabbed both sides of my head. "What happened? Did you get attacked by an old mop? It seems to have taken over your head."

I waited for some sassy reply about my body odor or my pea-sized brain. But Zoe just smoothed her hand through her ponytail and smiled.

"Yeah, it was quite a fight, but I found some good conditioner. So, I'm good. How was your day, dear brother? I hope it was great."

Oh, no!

If I couldn't get a rise out of my sister when I made fun of her hair, then the whole world had gone whack.

CHAPTER 2

Strange Smells

L oopy! Come here, boy!" I dropped my backpack and held out both hands, ready for my chocolate-colored Shih-poo, Loopy, to run down the stairs, jump into my arms, and drool me up. Like usual.

"Loopy?"

Nothing. No panting, jumping, or drooling. No Loopy!

Goosebumps covered my arms as I thought back to last fall when Loopy disappeared for a couple of months. In the *Internet*.

"LOOPY!" I ran to the kitchen, expecting to find him with his head in his dog dish.

Nope.

"Zoe! Loopy's gone!"

Zoe placed her backpack on the dining room table, strolled into the kitchen, and opened the refrigerator. She pulled out a flavored water. "He's not in there." She closed the door, unscrewed the cap, and took a few gulps. She came over and put a hand on my shoulder. "Don't worry about it, bro. Loopy's probably hiding upstairs waiting for you to take a shower." She sniffed. "I don't know what you've been doing at school lately, but it's got you smelling kinda . . . ripe."

Okay, now that's more like my sister.

I sniffed my underarm and cringed. "We've been playing volleyball in last period P.E. I've been sweating every day inside our hot gym in the middle of winter! Plus, I'm *almost* twelve, ya know. Sweat glands are working overtime."

Zoe didn't even crack a smile when I dropped the subtle birthday hint.

"Volleyball, huh? That's cool. What's your specialty? Setting, digging, or spiking?"

I shook my head. "I'm pretty much the person who wipes up the floor, since I'm always down there."

"Diving for the ball?"

"I'd call it more like tripping and falling after the ball. Casey Tolley keeps sticking his foot out in front of me. We're supposed to be on the same team."

"Do you want me to talk to Michael about it?"

"NO! That would make it worse."

Michael Tolley is Zoe's new boyfriend. He's the older brother of Kevin and Casey, and he obviously sapped all the nice genes out of the family when he was born.

Zoe shrugged. "Okay, then. Don't say I never tried to help."

I grabbed a sports drink out of the refrigerator. "And on Monday, they're mixing us up with the girls' P.E. class. We're playing in a tournament."

Zoe grinned. "Sounds like more humiliation is on the way for you."

"Well, at least I'll have a fun birthday weekend to look back on when I'm wiping up the floor."

Zoe ignored my comment and finished chugging her flavored water. "Mom and Dad will be home soon. I should get going on my homework."

"But it's Friday. You've got all weekend."

Zoe picked up her backpack and swung it over her shoulders. "You middle-schoolers clearly have *no idea* just how much work high school is." She waved and headed for the stairs. *"Au revoir, mon frère!"*

I reached my hands out. "But . . . Loopy! And remember tomorrow's my birthd—"

Just then, Doug blasted through the front door. "Arcade! I'm the MAN! I got everything I needed ON SALE! Not only am I the Food Dude, I got real shopping skills! CHA-CHING! Boy, aren't you glad I'm gonna be your brother."

Doug hoisted his shopping bag onto the counter.

My stomach growled. "Are you making dinner tonight?"

Doug tilted his head. "Am I making dinner tonight?'

"That's what I said."

He reached in the bag and pulled out some flour. "Nah. I got a food project."

"Are you making me a cake?" I asked with a little wiggle of my eyebrows.

"A cake?"

"Yeah, a cake."

He pulled out a bag of sugar. "Why would I make you a cake?" He leaned forward and sniffed. "Are *you* cooking dinner? Cause you smell like onions."

I raised my arms. "No onions. You can thank volleyball for the smell."

Doug scrunched his nose. "Dude, you better go take a sh—"

I held my hands up. "I'M GOING!"

I thumped up the stairs and flung open the door of the room that Doug and I had been sharing since November. Loopy was snoozing on the lower bunk. We added bunk beds after Christmas, rock-paper-scissored for the top, and Doug won.

"Hey, Loop! No wonder you didn't come down to greet me. Why are you in here with the door closed?" I sat down next to him.

"Oh, man. I'm sorry, boy. Have you been in here all day? Come here, let me give you a snuggle . . ."

Loopy sat up, sneezed, jumped off the bed, and ran under it.

"You too? Come on, I can't smell *that* bad."

I stood up and stripped off my shirt. Around my neck hung my Triple T Token. An old woman gave it to me at the library soon after my family moved to New York City, and ever since, it had been taking Zoe, me, and my friends on adventures through mysterious elevator doors. The last adventure had taken place the day after Thanksgiving, when the elevator took us to China to return a flamingo named Flames to the Beijing Zoo. I missed the little shrimp hog.

I looked at Loopy. "Hey, at least I don't smell like shrimp anymore." He poked his head out from under the bed.

"You think I stink?" I put my nose under one arm and took a big whiff. "Ugh. I guess it's true, then."

As soon as I said that, the Triple T Token, which had stayed cool and silent for almost two months, began to flash brilliant lights around the room.

CHAPTER 3

Seeing the Light

"ZOE! COME IN HERE! IT'S AN EMERGENCY!"

Loopy ran out from under the bed and chased after the light patterns that swirled around on my floor. He even jumped to try and bite the ones on the wall.

Zoe burst through the doorway. "WHAT? Arcade, are you all right?" She stood, frozen, staring at my token. "What the . . . OH, NOOOOO!"

I looked toward the ceiling, expecting what normally came next when the token came to life.

"Where's the glitter?" Zoe stood with one fist jammed into her hip.

"Maybe it only appears if the token heats up."

Zoe came over and touched the token. "It's cool." Then she examined the patterns on the wall. "But it's sure creating a dazzling display. What did you do to it?"

I shrugged. "Nothing."

Zoe adjusted her reading glasses on her face. She moved closer to the token, picking it up off my chest, and turning it around to examine the back, where "Arcade Adventures" was stamped across the bottom.

"Think, Arcade. Did you say anything before this all started?"

"I was just talking with Loopy."

"What did he say, Loopy?" She ran around until she caught him. She brought him up close to me. Loopy barked.

"Loopy told me I stink."

Zoe petted his head. "You are a smart doggy."

"And then I said, 'Ugh, I guess it's true then.'"

"HA! You admitted the truth!"

"Yeah! So what?"

Zoe shrugged. "I don't know. I just like you to admit I'm right once in a while." Her eyes widened. "Hey, maybe that's what triggered the token! You're finally seeing the wisdom in EVERYTHING I SAY."

I shook my head and waved my hands. "Now wait a minute, Zoe. That is NOT why this thing came to life. You have some of the weirdest ideas that I've ever heard."

I barely got that out of my mouth when the token stepped up the light show a hundred percent. Light prisms took over the room.

I squinted. "I'm gonna need my shades for this."

Zoe, who usually scowls and screams and complains when the token comes to life, danced around instead this time. "This is amaaaaaazing! You're seeing the light, Arcade! Zoe's truth about the world! I can't wait to see where we're going!" She ran over to my dresser and grabbed my spray deodorant. "Apply this, please. I don't want to regret one minute of this adventure."

I took the can, lifted my arm, and sprayed. Nothing came out. Zoe flew to my closet and pulled out a clean, red T-shirt.

"Here, at least put this on."

When she closed the closet door, it turned into a sparkling-gold elevator door. A golden coin slot rose up out of my floor, this time with a sign attached that said GET TRUTH.

I reached for the token, pulled, and it came off my chain into my hand. I turned to Zoe. "So, you good with this?"

Her eyes reflected the brilliant rays coming off the token. "Oh, yeah. I have a feeling I'm gonna love this."

I approached the coin slot. "Okay then, no complaining when you find out I'm right about *everything* in life."

"Ha." She pointed to the sign. "It says GET TRUTH. I'm sure I won't be complaining."

I held Triple T right above the slot but hesitated.

"What?" Zoe threw her hands up.

"We haven't been on a Triple T adventure for a while."

Zoe reached over and smacked the top of my hand, causing the token to drop directly into the coin slot. "Let's see what all this light is about."

Light streams shot through the cracks of the elevator doors. I had to shield my eyes.

"Make the open-door motion!" Zoe yelled.

"Oh yeah. Almost forgot about that!" I put my palms together and then pulled them apart. The doors opened. The light was unleashed. It was brilliant, but for some reason, it didn't make me want to jump back. It made me want to climb in.

Woof! Loopy appeared by my side as I took a step toward the elevator entrance.

"Loopy, last time you went through, you got lost! I'm not risking that again." I picked him up and placed him on my bed. "I'll be back for you, I promise." I jumped in the elevator, where Zoe was holding a golden handrail and staring at the dazzling lights all over the walls.

"Let's hope we aren't the ones who get lost this time," I said.

The elevator door closed.

Triple T elevators are tricky. Sometimes there's a button with only one choice. Sometimes there's one button with many choices. A few times, I had one button with no choices, so I shouted a command out loud. I'd learned the hard way to be careful what you ask for.

This time, there were no buttons at all! Just this golden sign at the top that said GET TRUTH.

"So, what're you gonna do, Einstein?" Zoe had one hand on her hip, and the other rubbing her neck.

I pointed to the sign. "I guess I'm going to ask it to show me the truth."

"The truth? About what?"

I grabbed hold of my golden chain that, just a few minutes ago, held the biggest mystery of my life over the last year.

The Triple T Token.

"I wanna know where the token goes every time I drop it in the slot."

And then *we* dropped.

"AAAAAHHHHHHHH! ARCAAAAAAADE!" Zoe screamed as the elevator plummeted. "Why did you SAAAAAY THAAAAAT?"

I reached for the golden doors to steady myself. "BECAUSE I REALLY WANT TO KNOW!!!!!"

"BUT WE'RE DROPPING!"

"I KNOW THAT! MAYBE THE TOKEN GOES TO ANTARCTICA!"

"ANTARCTICA?"

"YEAH, THAT WOULD BE DOPE!"

"NO, IT WOULD NOT BE DOPE!"

"WOULD TOO!"

"WOULD NOT!"

Right in the middle of the argument that was going nowhere, the elevator began to slow, as if a parachute had opened up on top. It eased to a stop.

Zoe and I stood there, staring at each other. The doors didn't open.

"Great. They're stuck." Zoe felt along the cracks of the doors that were still gold but had now turned an antique gold.

"Patience, Zoe. Remember your goal."

My sister Zoe and I set goals back in August for the school year. Zoe's was to grow in patience. Mine was to grow in compassion. I'm still working on it, especially with Zoe.

Zoe stepped back from the door. "Okay. Open when ready, ancient doors."

The doors creaked and slid open.

CHAPTER 4

The Beginning

Radiant sunlight streams through the doors. It's warm. I step out.

Zoe rubs her upper arms. "Well, good. It's not Antarctica."

We're at the top of a large, outdoor amphitheater. The seats are made of white stone. There's a stage at the bottom of the many rows. Behind the stage is a stunning crystal blue sea. A few small boats float in the distance.

Zoe and I take a few steep steps down to the middle of the amphitheater. Zoe shields her eyes as she looks out at the ocean. "This is where the token goes? I don't get it."

"Check it out, Zoe." I point toward several rows of white stone arches on our right.

Zoe smiles. "Arcades."

"What?"

"Arcades."

"I heard you. What?"

"What?" She crunches her eyebrows together. "Oh, did you think I was calling *you*?"

"Well, you said my name."

She throws her head back in frustration. "I'm saying that *those* . . ." she holds her hand out to the arches, "are ARCADES. A series of arches is called an arcade. You should know that. Check it out." She turns in a complete circle. "They're all around us."

She's right. Arcades everywhere.

I turn back to the ocean view and notice two people sitting way down in the front row of the amphitheater. One appears to be a boy about my size, and another is a woman of small build, wearing what looks like a ball cap and a white sweat suit.

I jet down the steps of the amphitheater.

"ARCADE!" Zoe yells.

"I know! They're everywhere."

"NO! This time I *am* calling you. Wait up!"

I don't stop. I have to get a closer look at the two people in the front row. Within eight rows of them, I trip over the uneven stone. I watch from the ground as the boy stands, hugs the lady, glances at me, and disappears into the sun's blinding rays. I scramble the rest of the way, finally reaching her. She turns to look at me. I freeze.

"Uh . . . oh . . . I'm sorry. I thought you were . . ." I crane my neck forward and examine her face closely.

She smiles. "It's me, Arcade."

I put my hand over my mouth to stifle a gasp. She's wearing the Triple T ball cap, but she's . . . young.

Like, Zoe-young! In fact, she even kinda looks like Zoe. I sit down next to her. "Uh . . . you're . . ."

"Younger. Yes, I know. This is the real me."

"The real you?"

"Yes. The other way is just how you perceive me."

I stare down at her white running shoes. "Well, I always wondered how you could move so fast."

She laughs.

"ARCADE!" It's Zoe. She's still many rows up, waving a shoe in the air. I know I should go check on my sister, but the Triple T lady makes only brief visits, so I stay put.

"Do you have a name?"

The woman grins. "Ruah."

I glance down at a hunk of metal Ruah is holding in her lap.

"In the elevator that brought me here, I asked to know where the token goes when I put it in the coin slot. Is it in there?"

She pulls off the top of the metal piece, and there it sits. In a mold! It's the same mold I saw at a gold refinery where the Triple T Token was cast in one hundred percent pure gold. Ruah was there too.

Ruah glances out in the distance. The boy who left a few moments ago is scrambling over some rocks, heading to what looks like a cluster of homes.

"ARCADE! MY SHOE BROKE! DON'T YOU CARE?"

I care about Zoe, but not her shoes. That pair, in particular.

"Where is he going?" I ask, pointing to the boy just as he disappears over the other side of the rocks.

"Back to work." Ruah frowns. "Every day. Back to work."

"Work?" I scratch my head. "But he's my age."

"He's *exactly* your age." Ruah holds up the mold. "And a craftsman. He made this."

"*That boy* made the Triple T mold?" My heart beats faster.

Ruah stands up, takes the token out of the mold, and drops it in my hand. It lights up. Gleaming, but not hot, yet somehow warming me on the inside. Ruah puts her hand over the dazzling token. "Use it well, Arcade. You have traveled, and you have been tested."

"Yeah. About that testing. Do you know how hard it is to take care of a baby flamingo?"

Ruah chuckled. "Now you are free to experience the widest, the longest, the highest, and the deepest."

"The widest what? The deepest what?"

Ruah nods. "Yes. You're getting it now."

"GETTING WHAT?"

The glittery Triple Ts on Ruah's ball cap shoot out rays of light. I shield my eyes.

"Arcade!" Zoe jumps down from the row above me and holds up her shoe. "I fixed it. With no help from you, of course." She sits down and pokes me in the side with her elbow.

I stare in front of me, trying to see past the flashes in my eyes, but Ruah isn't there anymore.

"Arcade?" Zoe looks around. "Why did you take off? Why didn't you wait for me?"

"She was down here."

"*Who* was down here?"

"Ruah."

Zoe rubs her neck with both hands. "Okay, I'll play your game. Who's Ruah?"

"The Triple T woman. That's her name."

"Of course. Ruah! That's a pretty name. Did you catch her *last* name? You know, so we can look her up on the Internet and find out where she lives? Maybe she's on social media."

I turn to Zoe with a questioning gaze. "Are you serious?"

She gives me a little shove. "No."

"Good." I hold up the token. "Because I think she lives in this thing."

As soon as I say that, the token dazzles light, sparkling like the sun reflecting off the ocean. It summons the antique elevator doors to the amphitheater stage. The coin slot, with the GET TRUTH sign attached, rises up from the ground.

I sigh. "Guess it's time to go home."

Zoe glares at me. "DO NOT SAY THE WORD *DROP*."

"What would you like me to say?"

"Say the word . . ." Zoe puts one hand to her chin and sniffs, "shower."

The trip back is slow. I study the inside of the elevator. "What in the world . . .?"

Zoe tilts her head and her jaw drops open. "Whoa. That's a beautiful ceiling. It's never been like this before."

The ceiling is a huge, gold dome with signs that are way, way up. I squint through my super-strong, long-distance glasses.

"Zoe, can you read the signs?"

Zoe takes off her glasses—which she mostly needs for reading—rises up on her tip-toes, and squints. "No. And it's really bugging me. I bet they say something profound."

"Profound?"

"Well, yeah. The words look like they're carved into the gold. Who would take the time to carve something *unimportant* into gold?"

I pull my phone out of my pocket. "Maybe I can take a picture and enlarge it."

"Nope. Phones don't work in your token world, Arcade. Remember? You should mention that inconvenience to Ruah next time you see her."

I lower my phone, which is showing me nothing but

flashing lights on the screen. "So how am I supposed to see what's up there?"

"Beats me. Grow taller, I guess."

"Oh, well you know, that could happen soon, since tomorrow is my bir—"

DING!

The doors opened on their own, and Loopy was right there waiting, panting and slobbering.

Woof!

I turned to Zoe. "That was an interesting trip. I'm glad we didn't get lost, but something about me feels lost all of a sudden."

"What do you mean, *lost?*"

I shrug. "I don't know. Maybe 'confused' is a better word. And that boy sure is a mystery."

"What boy?"

"The boy scrambling over the rocks. He was talking to Ruah, and then he left. Ruah said he was going back to work."

"Work?"

"Yeah. She told me that *he's* the one who made the mold for the Triple T Token!"

Zoe grabbed me by the T-shirt sleeve. "Get over here." She pulled me over to my desk chair. "Arcade, what did you ask right before you put the token in the slot this time?"

"Uh . . ." I scratched my head and tried to clear the blur

from my brain. I looked down at my token, which was once again hanging from the gold chain around my neck. "I asked to know where this thing goes when I put it in the slot."

"And did you find out?"

"Well, I saw the token. Ruah put it back in my hand after she took it out of the mold."

"So, if we just 'Got Truth,' that would mean . . ."

"That the token goes back to the mold every time?"

"It goes back to its origin. The beginning. That makes sense."

I stood and paced the room. "No, that doesn't make sense at all! A mold is just a thing. Why would a token that seems to be alive go back to a dead mold? Why would the mold care?"

Zoe joined me in the pacing. "It wouldn't. But the maker of the mold might."

I gasped and grabbed the token. "THAT makes sense!"

Zoe pushed me in the arm. "Now you're seeing things my way."

"Zoe, I need to go to the library."

She rolled her eyes. "So, tell me something new."

I grabbed my flamingo backpack. "I need to find out about ancient Greece. About metalworkers. And I need to find that boy."

Zoe grabbed my backpack strap. "Hold up, Skippy."

"What?"

"It's dinner time. You'll have to go tomorrow."

"Oh, man." I put my backpack back on the desk. "I guess that'll work. I'm going with the Tolleys tomorrow anyway."

"The Tolleys?" Zoe chuckled. "Really, Arcade? Has your life gotten so boring that now you're choosing to hang out with Kevin and Casey?"

"Hey, they invited me. And no one else has invited me to do anything tomorrow. Which is whack, since it's my bir—"

"Arcade! Zoe! Dinner!"

Mom's voice from the bottom level of our brownstone echoed up the stairs.

"Arcade! Zoe! Dinner!"

And that voice . . . was Doug's.

CHAPTER 5

It's my Bir—

don't want to work . . . I want to learn . . ."

"Learning is work, Arcade."

"I get that, but . . . hey, what do these gold signs say?"

"The signs contain quotes about knowledge, wisdom, and truth."

"Aren't those all the same thing?"

"Sometimes."

"Sometimes? That's not an answer."

"But it's the kind of answer you appreciate."

"You're right. But why? Why am I like that?"

"Because the truth about you is . . ."

All of a sudden, I couldn't breathe! I opened my eyes and gasped. Loopy had stretched out to sleep with me in my bed. One leg was resting over my mouth. The other one was plugging my nose! I pushed him off. "Loopy!" I sneezed. "You interrupted my dream! I was about to find out the truth about myself!"

Doug stirred on the top bunk. "Arcade, dude, can you find out the truth about yourself later? It's Saturday, man, and I really wanted to sleep in. I was dreaming of chicken parmesan!"

I jumped out of bed. "Doug! I just had a crazy dream! I was floating inside a golden dome, and there were paintings and sculptures all around me."

Doug rubbed his eyes, stretched, and yawned. "Sounds cool. But not as cool as chicken parm."

I shook him. "And there were golden plaques all around, but I couldn't read 'em, cause it was blurry." I grabbed my glasses off my dresser and shoved them on my face. "Hey, Doug, do you think my dreams are blurry 'cause I don't wear my glasses when I sleep?"

"I have NO idea. Ask the eye doc next time you're there." Doug turned over to face the wall.

"DOUG! Zoe and I went on an elevator trip last night, and there was a golden dome at the top—the ceiling. It was the same dome as in my dream!"

Doug sat up, swung his legs over the bed, and jumped down. "You went on another Arcade adventure? Where did you go? Were there flames and intense heat like last time?"

"No. No heat. Just blinding light. We went to Greece!"

"Greece! You went to *Greece* without me?"

"Well, I think it was Greece. I'm going to research it at the library today. I'm sure Ms. Weckles—"

Doug put his hand on my shoulder. "No! You can't go to the library today."

I stepped back. "Really? Why not? The Tolleys invited me."

Doug crossed his arms over his pajama top with the pizza-slice pattern. He shifted his eyes left, then right. "Oh, wait. Yep. My bad. You can go."

"Just like that? You sure changed your mind fast. What's goin' on, Doug?"

"Nothin'. I'm just tired and confused. Yeah. You need to go with the Tolleys. It's the library. You're a bookworm. It will make you happy. What time are you going again?"

I just stared at him. "Two o'clock."

Doug checked an invisible watch on his wrist. "Two o'clock. Right. That's right. And with the Tolleys. Yep. That's a plan. I'll see you later."

And then he ran out the door. In his pajamas.

I looked at Loopy, who was standing and panting, watching Doug tear out of there.

Woof!

"Yeah, I know, boy. Happy birthday to me." I sniffed. "Hey, Loop, do you smell chocolate chip pancakes?"

I ran down the stairs. "Happy January twenty-second, everybody!" I threw my arms up in a victory pose, but there was nobody around. I must have been imagining the aroma of the birthday pancakes Mom usually makes for me, because there wasn't any action happening in the kitchen. Doug wasn't even in there.

Where did he go so fast?

I plunked down on the couch. Mom stepped in the front door wearing her winter workout clothes and carrying some mail. She shivered as she closed the door. "Brrrr. It's chilly out there. But I had a fabulous jog this morning! Saw lots of friends in Central Park." She sorted through the envelopes in her hands. "Arcade, you have a couple of letters."

I jumped up off the couch to retrieve them. "Thanks! They look like cards for my bir—"

"MOM! COME QUICK! I NEED YOU!"

Zoe.

Mom's eyes widened. "Whoa. Sounds urgent." She ran up the stairs.

"But MOM! I need you too!" I stroked my chin. "I think I'm sprouting a beard hair!"

I carried my mail over to the dining room table. A small envelope sat there with my name on it. It was in Dad's handwriting. Dad was upstairs sleeping. He gets home early every morning from his job as a set designer and stage manager on Broadway.

"Good old Dad. I'm sure *he* remembered my birthday." I put down the other two envelopes and opened Dad's. It was one of his famous notes. He leaves them for me and Zoe since he can't always greet us in the morning.

> "What doth the Lord require of thee, but to do justly, and to love mercy, and to walk humbly with thy God?" Micah 6:8 KJV.
> Great thing to ponder, right, Arcade?
> Mom and I have a long errand to run this afternoon. Hopefully we will be home by dinner. Have a great day . . . and walk humbly!
> —Dad

I read the note three times. Doth? Thee?

"Well, Loop, this *is* a great verse to ponder, but it looks like Dad forgot my birthday too." I turned around and around. "Loop?"

I ran upstairs and watched from the hallway as Loopy scooted back into my bedroom.

Mom came out of Zoe's room, brushing her hands together. "Crisis averted! Oh, good, you're here, Arcade. I have to go out this morning, and then I'm meeting your dad for an errand this afternoon. I'll grab lunch in the city. Are you all set with everything you need for today? Doug mentioned that you were going to the library with the Tolleys at two o'clock. I think it's very nice that you've befriended those boys. You can be a good influence on them."

"Yeah, I love to be a good influence, but today is my birthday," is what I *wanted* to say. But Mom was down the stairs and out the front door before I had the chance.

What's goin' on here?

I knocked on Zoe's door. A perturbed sister voice came from behind it.

"If that's you, Arcade, it's going to have to wait. I've got some issues that need attention."

"What, more broken shoes?" I whispered, turning in a huff.

Well, when your people and your dog desert you, there's always good old snail mail.

I started down the stairs to retrieve my two letters.

"Arcade's a mess! Arcade's a mess!"

I glared at my sister's cockatoo, Milo, who was swinging in his cage that hangs from the ceiling of our living room.

"Yeah, well, you're looking pretty ragged yourself, Milo."

"Zoe's the best! Zoe's the best!"

My sister loves to teach her bird phrases that get me all riled up.

"Come on, Milo, say 'Happy birthday, Arcade!'"

"Zoe's the best! Zoe's the best!"

I resisted the urge to let Milo outside to fly with the wild New York City birds. Instead, I focused on my mail.

The first piece was a birthday card from my grandparents with a twenty-dollar bill inside. "Aww, you guys you didn't have to do that!" I ran my fingers over the raised purple number twelve on the card. They had written a message inside.

Dear Favorite Grandson Arcade,

(They say that to whichever grandson they're with at the time.)

Twelve is a special year. Make the most of it! It's your last year to be a child. Discover your true self now, and when you do, you'll never forget it! Even when the teen years confuse you.

"Ha! This explains why Zoe is so confused."

"Zoe's the best! Zoe's the best!"

"Quiet, Milo."

The next envelope made my stomach jump. It was from Miss Gertrude in Virginia! Miss Gertrude has known me since I was a kid. She's also the grandma of Lenwood and Kenwood Badger, brothers who once owned the Triple T Token. One time they tried to take the token from me, and they ended up stuck in San Francisco. In 1935. They're back in the present day now . . . I'm just not exactly sure where. Miss Gertrude was at the hospital on the day I was born. An elevator took us there once, and Zoe and I watched her steal the Triple T Token from my mom. I paused at the memory.

Why did you do that, Miss Gertrude?

This card was the same one my grandparents sent— with the raised purple number twelve. Miss Gertrude also included a message.

Happy Birthday, Arcade. Keep shining your dazzling light in the world. "As one lamp lights another, nor grows less, so nobleness enkindleth nobleness."

Sincerely, Gertrude

She had taped twelve dollars in the card. One dollar for each year. Sweet!

Note to self. At the library today, look up "enkindleth."

Miss Gertrude had drawn a squiggly arrow on the bottom of the card's insert paper. I turned the paper over.

P.S. They are back.

I dropped the twelve bucks *and* the card. I put my head in my hands. "OH, NO! THEY'RE BACK! THE BADGERS ARE BACK!"

"The Badgers are back! The Badgers are back! Happy birthday, Arcade!"

"Not NOW, Milo! I'm in real trouble here!"

The Badgers are back. And no one in this house remembers it's my birthday except Milo.

CHAPTER 6

Library Hunt

I was relieved to meet the Tolley brothers at two o'clock. It took my mind off worrying that the Badger brothers could be in my neighborhood right now, plotting to overpower me and steal the token.

Not today! Not on my birthday!

"Hey, Arcade? You alright? I thought this was your favorite place to chill." Casey nudged me out of my thoughts in front of the library aquarium.

"Huh? Oh, yeah. This place is great. And I'm sure Ms. Weckles will help us find what you're looking for." I stared at the fish and imagined seeing a face in the water. The face of Lenwood Badger. He had stalked me before in the library when my friend Scratchy and I were here. He also stole Daisy—that suitcase I use to carry all the library books I get. I pulled her in a little closer. "What is it you guys are looking for again?"

Kevin sighed. "We told you on the way over. Civil War stuff. For our persuasive essays. Man, did you hear anything we said on the subway?"

"I told you he was zonin' the whole time." Casey pulled

Kevin aside and whispered something in his ear. A very un-Tolley-like thing to do, but whatever. It gave me a chance to flag down the children's librarian, Ms. Weckles.

"Arcade! It's great to see you, as usual."

"Hello, Ms. Weckles. I see you got some new fish."

She came over and wiped some finger smudges off the glass with a cloth. "Yes, we had to. Puffer ate a few of the striped damselfish. Seems certain saltwater varieties can't coexist in the same tank. I guess we should have been reading some of our own books about saltwater fish. Puffers are aggressive."

"Why don't you get rid of *him*?"

"Well, he's been here the longest, so it's his home. Kids love the puffer."

"But he's prickly and mean."

"Yes, but he's interesting."

"Ahem, we don't have all day, bookworm," said Kevin. Speaking of prickly . . .

"Well, hello, Kevin and Casey. What brings you into the library today?" Ms. Weckles asked with a big smile and no hint of sarcasm at all.

"Arcade did." Casey laughed. "He's an expert on this place, and we need Civil War stuff. You got anything like that around here?" Casey looked around with a blank stare. "My brother and I are doing persuasive essays. One from the North's point of view, one from the South's."

Ms. Weckles walked over to one of the computer kiosks and started entering information. "That's an excellent idea! You know that during the Civil War, depending on where they lived, brothers sometimes had to fight brothers?"

"Yeah, we kinda know how that works."

Kevin gave Casey a little shove as they followed Ms. Weckles to the American history shelves.

Now's my chance!

I ducked into the travel aisle, where I had first met Ruah. I pulled Daisy along with me. I laid her down on the floor and piled in all the books I could find about Greece. I hoped that one of them would have pictures that would match where the token had taken me and Zoe. An old amphitheater, with arcades in the distance, and a crystal blue ocean . . .

"ARCADE! Where'd you go?"

One of the Tolleys had forgotten to use his library voice. He thundered around the corner and gave me the stink eye.

"Whatcha doin' down there on the floor? Our books are over *here*." He jerked his thumb over his shoulder. "Ms. Weckles found a boatload for us."

"Um, okay. Just a minute. I'm getting some books too."

"Nah. You can leave 'em. You won't have room in there with all of ours."

"But you don't need . . ."

Kevin came around the corner, his arms loaded down with books. "There's so much on the Civil War! And Ms. Weckles says we're gonna study this next year in eighth grade, so we're gettin' a head start on knowing everything."

I stood up and adjusted my glasses. "Knowledge is a fun thing. That's why I was going to pick up a few books on—"

"Nah, we don't have time," Kevin frowned. "We gotta be somewhere at four."

"Four? You didn't tell me that."

"Oh, we sure did, Arcade Livingston. In the subway when you were all doo-doo-doo . . ." Casey crossed his eyes and acted dizzy. "Some of us got a life, ya know."

Kevin chuckled. "Yeah. An exciting life. Let's go."

So the Tolleys had a life. And somewhere exciting to go. *But why don't I?*

Nothing surprised me more than seeing the Tolley brothers whip out their library cards. Kevin approached the checkout counter first, and the librarian complimented him on his stack of books. "This was a fascinating time in American history. When you're done with these, we have a whole section of historical fiction on this topic as well."

"Fiction? About the Civil War? How does that work?"

"Well, the characters are made up, but the events surrounding their story match up to real history."

"Really? I didn't know books could work that way."

"Books are the bomb," I said.

Kevin finished his checkout, and Casey was next. "Where do I find that . . . what did you call it? Historical fiction? We studied about the Revolutionary War in fifth grade. You got any fiction on that?"

The librarian grinned. "We have fiction on every topic. You'll love the stories, and you'll learn a lot too."

Casey took his stack and started stuffing it into Daisy.

"Any room for these?" I pointed to my small stack of books on Greece.

Casey looked up. "You're in luck. We can fit 'em."

I handed my library card to the librarian, and she scanned it. "Arcade Livingston? You have a block on your account."

"A block?!? Must be some mistake. I never have a block."

"You have two *very* overdue books."

I shook my head. "No, I turn all my books in on time. Even early. There was only one time when I was late, when a guy stole my books, but I got an extension, and I returned each one."

The woman's serious expression didn't change. "The overdue titles are *French Decorating* and *The Care and Feeding of Today's Cockatoo.*"

ZOE!

"Those are my sister's books."

"But they're checked out under your card."

"Yeah, I know, we were here together. She forgot her card, so I checked them out for her."

"Arcade, we gotta go, man." Kevin wheeled Daisy toward the door.

I held my hand out. "One minute." I turned back to the librarian. "I'm sure if you check my past records, you'll see that I'm an excellent library patron."

She smiled. "I'm sure you are. Unfortunately, unless you have these two books with you, or you can pay the replacement fee today, you can't check out any more books."

"Arcade . . ." Casey inched toward the door.

"Hey, Casey, can I use your card for these books?"

Casey got a horrified look on his face. "Are you kiddin'? You're a library delinquent! I don't want my record messed up. I need to come back and check out some of that historical fiction." He turned and walked out the door.

"Would you like me to keep these here for you? I can place an unofficial hold for forty-eight hours."

"Uh, okay. Maybe Monday after school I can make it ba—"

"Oh, wait." The librarian read something on her computer screen. "This is so strange, but someone just placed a hold on all of these books. I guess people are curious about Greece these days."

"Can I put a hold on them for when that person is done with them?"

"I'm sorry, but no. That would be an official hold, and

you can't put an official hold on a book if you have a block on your account."

I glanced over at Casey. He was gone.

"This is my worst library nightmare, you know." My shoulders drooped.

"I'm so sorry. I feel your pain. I love books too." She looked at her screen again. "But hey, I have something that might cheer you up."

"You're gonna lift the block?"

She laughed. "No. But it says here on your record that you were born on January twenty-second." She reached into a basket behind the desk, pulled out a book-shaped sucker, and handed it to me. "Happy birthday, Arcade."

I took it, pulled off the wrapper, and stuck it in my mouth. "Thanks. I'll be back to clear my good name. Now please excuse me as I go find my delinquent sister."

She smiled. "See you soon."

I caught up to the Tolley brothers just as they were about to carry Daisy down the stairs to the subway.

"What's wrong with you, Arcade? You're all doo-doo-doo again. We gotta get you home." When Casey said that, Kevin gave him a weird look.

"You gotta get *me* home? Why?"

"Oh, well, you gotta find those overdue books!"

Since when do the Tolleys care so much about library books?

CHAPTER 7

Big Surprises

asey and Kevin walked me all the way up the steps of my brownstone and right to my door.

"Just need to get our books out of your suitcase and we're outta here," Kevin said while Casey nodded.

I opened the door, wanting nothing more than for this day to be over, when the cheers erupted.

"SURPRISE! HAPPY BIRTHDAY, ARCADE!"

WHAT?!?

My mom, dad, Zoe, and Doug were all standing there smiling and clapping. Zoe grabbed my hand and pulled me to the dining room, where a huge cake shaped like a book was waiting for me.

"You like my food project, Arcade?" Doug asked as he began lighting the candles on top. "I stayed up half the night working on this thing! I used fondant, and I didn't even eat it this time."

It was awesome! A cake, shaped like a thick book, opened to the middle. It said *Arcade's Life*, and there was a red number twelve at the bottom.

I inched a little closer to check out the masterpiece. "Doug, you're amazing!"

"What about us?" I turned around. The Tolleys were standing right behind me in the dining room. "We were in on this the whole time."

The Tolleys?

And then the singing started. At first, it was just Mom, Dad, Doug, and Zoe, with some grunts from the Tolleys. But then a few others came from the kitchen and joined in. They sang off-key, but I didn't care, because it was my cousins from Virginia, Celeste and Derek!

And Jacey Green. The girl I met at the Bridgeview Bakery. She and her family helped us rebuild the windmill course at Forest Games and Golf—the business the Badger brothers own.

"Hi, Arcade." Her smile beamed. "Happy birthday. I've always wanted to visit New York City."

My cheeks got hot.

This is crazy sauce!

There was a lot of high-fiving, hugging, and fist bumping. "Dude! Did we surprise you, or what?" Derek popped off his yellow upside-down visor and placed it on my head. "This is a cool city you got here!"

"Yeah, Arcade." My cousin Celeste came over and punched me in the arm. "And we only have one day, so you have to hurry and show us *everything*."

"Only one day?" I glanced over at Mom and Dad.

"Sorry, bud," Dad said. "It was all we could wrangle with school schedules and everything."

"Okay, then, let's get started. This is the city that never sleeps, so that gives us some hours."

Mom brought some paper plates over to the table. "First you should blow out these candles. The wax is ruining Doug's artwork."

"Oh, yeah!" I stood behind the cake.

"Make a good wish, Arcade. It's the last one of your childhood." The way Zoe said that made me think about the boy in Greece who had made the Triple T mold. We were connected somehow, through time and travel. And, I suspected, through testing too. What had Ruah said?

You are ready to experience the widest, the longest, the highest, the deepest . . .

I grabbed my chest, hoping the token wasn't going to show off its brilliant display in front of everyone. I took a deep breath.

I wish to experience the -ESTS of life.

I exhaled and blew out all the candles. It wasn't so hard. There were only three.

The sounds of cheers and claps filled the room.

"Good job, brother. You always were full of hot air." Zoe laughed.

I grabbed the token under my shirt.

Where will we go next?

CHAPTER 8
The First -EST

You people can't see New York City until you experience my white chocolate raspberry swirl cake." Doug brought a knife and serving tools from the kitchen. "Arcade, you get the first taste. Man, this was hard to pull off with you in the house."

Doug cut out the big piece that had the twelve on it and plopped it on my plate. "Here you go. Happy birthday!" Doug handed it to me, beaming with pride.

"This is an amazing cake, Doug." I took a big bite. "And it's the best I've ever tasted! I think you could open a bakery now!"

"Well, he needs a lot of decorating training." Zoe took the knife from Doug and began serving. "But he did okay with a little help from me."

Mom came up behind me and put a hand on my shoulder. "She was working on the finishing touches all day in her room."

"Is *that* what the crisis was? I thought you were having a bad hair day again."

"Again? Hey, maybe *you* need a little help with *your* hair." Zoe pushed her finger into the raspberry swirl and came at me with it.

Casey Tolley laughed. "Hey, look, Kevin! They fight like we do."

"Yeah. That's cool. We'd love to stay around for the wrestling match, but we gotta go. Mom's cookin' dinner."

Casey took a step toward the cake table. "I wanna stay for the party."

"We gotta go!" Kevin put Casey in a headlock and pushed him toward the door. "Happy birthday, Arcade. We'll see you around."

I waved. "Thanks, guys."

They wrestled their way out. It was nice of them to help with my birthday surprise . . . but it's always a bit of a relief when the Tolleys leave.

Zoe got one smudge of raspberry swirl on my forehead before Dad stopped her. "That's enough." He held his index finger up in the air. "We're going out, so no food fights." He checked his watch. "We're leaving in twenty minutes. Don't forget to put on warm clothes." With that, he and Mom grabbed some cake plates and took off upstairs.

Doug licked frosting off his finger. "And I don't want any morsel of my cake wasted."

I took another bite. "That's the truth."

Just then, the token erupted with light. Flashing beams shot out from under my shirt, and two beams shot straight up into my eyes, dropping me to my knees. I put one hand out, keeping a tight grip on my cake plate with the other. "Zoe? Doug? Are you still here?"

I felt hands on my shoulders. "Arcade, are you all right?" It was Jacey. "Your token is putting on the most amazing light show!" She already knew about the token and had traveled with us to India, San Francisco, and Niagara Falls.

"Yeah. It's been doing that lately. But the lights hit me in the eyes and now I can't see anything! Can you guys see anything?"

"Yeah." Zoe took the cake plate out of my hand and pulled me to my feet. "I can see antique gold elevator doors and a coin slot, right here in our living room. Here we go again, bro!"

"Dude," Derek said, "and this time there's a sign above the coin slot!"

"No kidding?" I put both hands out in front of me and walked forward till I hit a barrier. "What does the sign say?"

"Just like before." Zoe came up behind me. "Get truth."

"Awesome! Quick, someone pull off my token and drop it in the slot." I felt a tug on my chain. Then another. And another.

"It's no use, Arcade." Zoe grabbed my hand and put the token in it. "*You* have to do it."

I clasped my fingers around Triple T and pulled. It came off, like it always does.

"But I can't see what I'm doing!"

"I'll help you." Zoe took my hand and placed it on top of the coin slot. "Okay, go ahead and let go."

I did. And then I heard squeaks and rolling, and gasps from everyone around me.

"This is magical," Jacey squealed. "They even look like doors I imagined New York City would have."

"Except they're pure gold," Doug said.

Man, I wish I could see!

I felt a bunch of hands grabbing my arms, my shoulders, and my shirt. They pulled me forward. Then more squeaks, telling me the doors were closing.

Ding!

The elevator was on the move. And my vision cleared!

"Whew, I thought I was blind for a second!" I reached both hands up to my glasses and was grateful for my vision, even if it had to be corrected with supersonic lenses.

"So, does this mean we aren't going to see New York City?" Celeste stood in the corner of the elevator, one hip sticking out, arms crossed, a frown on her face.

"Aw, c'mon, Sis." Derek nudged Celeste. "You know this is gonna be a good trip."

"Where do you think we're going, Arcade?" Zoe walked around inside the elevator, fingering the cracks in the gold. "Did you say anything to the token before you dropped it in the slot?" She pointed to the gold sign above the doors that said GET TRUTH.

"I was being blinded, so I don't remember. But—"

Derek jumped in next to me. "But what? Are we gonna meet the Badgers?" He held up his fists. "I got your back, cousin."

"No! I hope we don't run into them! Not now, at least.

I was going to say that I made a wish on the token before I blew out my candles."

Zoe stepped in close. "What was the wish?"

I pushed her away. "You're not supposed to tell people your birthday wishes."

She groaned.

"But it does have something to do with what Ruah said."

"Wait now. Who's Ruah?" Doug asked.

Zoe held her hand out. "No time to explain. Arcade, did your wish have anything to do with truth?"

"Yes," I said with a smirk. "You're getting it now."

"GETTING WHAT?"

I laughed. "Ruah said that. Can't you just wait and see, Zoe? We'll be there any minute."

"Where? Where will we be?" Jacey jumped up and down. "I loved when we went to India."

I tilted my head back and was just as surprised as the first time to see that magnificent gold dome again. "Hey, guys! Can you read what those signs say? Derek, you're tall—can you see them?"

Derek looked up. "Whoa!" He squinted and turned around a few times. "Nah, I can't quite make them out. Looks like there's a hole up in the top of that dome, though."

Celeste got a boost from Zoe and crawled up on Doug's shoulders. "I don't think that's a hole. It's a light. And it looks like there's a person up there! Could someone be watching us?"

My stomach lurched. Right then the elevator came to a halt. The antique doors squealed as they began to open.

"I hope you wished good, Arcade." Zoe wrung her hands, and then reached up to help Celeste down.

Goosebumps rose on my arms. "I did."

As the doors roll open, they unveil the most astonishing thing I've ever seen. Elephants, a herd of them, lumbering through a grassy plain, followed by giraffes, and . . . ostriches?

"Duuuuuuude! Are we in *Africa*?" Doug claps his hands to the sides of his face and steps out. Celeste, Jacey, and Derek follow. "Trip of a lifetime, man!"

I start to exit, but Zoe grabs me by the sleeve. "Don't get any crazy ideas. We're *not* taking any of those animals home." Then she sighs. "What am I saying? All your ideas are crazy."

I pull my sleeve out of Zoe's grip and step out of the elevator. The parade of animals continues through the long grass. "No worries, sis. They'll never fit in the elevator. The African elephant is the world's largest land mammal, and the giraffe is the tall . . . est."

Hey, wait a minute!

Doug stands there with his jaw hanging open. "This waaaaaay beats the Bronx Zoo!"

Jacey covers her cheeks with her hands. "They're beautiful. I could watch them all day!"

I look up and down at my outstretched arms. "Do you think they can see us? I mean, they aren't charging, and one time we were invisible."

"We could test it." Derek puts two fingers to his mouth and whistles.

"Derek!" Celeste pulls his hand from his mouth. "That's not the way to test it!"

But maybe it is. Because none of the animals turn to look at us.

"I want to get closer." Jacey holds her hand out to me. "Will you come with me, Arcade?"

Sweat squirts out of all the pores in my head.

What am I supposed to do? Say no? We are *in Africa and . . . well . . . she asked.*

I grab her hand and she, Zoe, and I walk out of the elevator toward the animal parade. We end up in the middle of a family of elephants. Doug, Celeste, and Derek check out the giraffes.

"They're huge, yet so calm and gentle." Jacey drops my hand and reaches out to pet one of the babies.

Zoe gasps. "That could be a problem if the mom doesn't want you doing that."

Jacey grins and rubs the baby's trunk. "He seems to like it." The larger elephants don't notice us. "I think we are invisible." She pets the baby on the head. "God sure had a great idea when he made you, little one." She looks around at the giraffes and ostriches and starts laughing. "And I thought I was going to New York City this weekend. Wait till I tell . . . oh, wait, I guess I can't tell anybody!"

"Yeah," Zoe says with a smile, "welcome to our world over the last year. Arcade's Triple T Token has been providing one rip-roaring, don't-tell-a-soul adventure after another."

"Do your parents know about it yet?" Jacey moves through the family of elephants toward the giraffes.

I follow. "The token? Maybe."

Jacey stops to look at me. "Maybe?"

"Our parents had the token long before Arcade did," Zoe explains. "They won it from the claw machine at Arcade Adventures. It was in there by mistake, and the Badger brothers were *not* happy to lose it."

I shake my head. "I don't think it was a mistake, Zoe."

Zoe ignored my comment. "So the answer is, yes, our parents know about the token. But, no, they don't know Arcade has it."

Jacey raises an eyebrow. "Are you *sure* they don't know?"

"I'm sure," I say. "If they knew, they'd put a stop to it for sure."

Jacey tilts her head. "Would they?"

I stop in my tracks. "What are you talking about?"

"Well, what if they know, but they want you to experience everything they did? Ooooh! I just had a crazy thought! What if they're somehow *watching us* right now?"

Zoe holds her hand out. "That's impossible. We'd see them."

"But *we're* invisible now, right?" Jacey rubs her arms and turns around.

Zoe's eyes widen. "Okay, stop. You're blowing my mind."

I get a chill up my spine. "Celeste did say she saw someone watching through the light in the elevator ceiling."

"Celeste saw a hole, or a light, and a blob she *thinks*

could be a person. It's a long shot! Plus, that ceiling hasn't shown up in the Triple T elevators until yesterday."

"At least that's been our perception," I say. "Ruah always looked old to me until yesterday. She said that's just how I've *perceived* her. Maybe the truth is—"

"The truth is, those ostriches need us to ride them!" Doug comes running over. "Look, Arcade, they're lined up in a row! And there's six of them! Wanna race?"

"Ha!" Zoe laughs. "Arcade hates birds!"

I push her away. "I do not. I just don't like Milo. May I remind you that one of my best friends is a flamingo?" I start walking toward the ostriches. "Did you know that the ostrich is the larges—"

An ostrich is an -EST. So is an elephant. So is a giraffe. This is DOPE!

"Sure, Doug, let's race!" I run up to the biggest of the birds, grab it by the feathers, and hoist myself up. Then I smooth its feathers. "There now, friend, why are you an -EST?" I turn to my friends. "It's okay! They really don't know we're here!"

Zoe scowls. "Arcade, this reminds me too much of our first token adventure! Remember Bone Crusher? I suggest you get down!"

"Well, maybe you should be the rodeo clown again! You still have your red nose?"

Celeste is the next brave one to jump on an ostrich. "C'mon, Zoe. I bet my ostrich can outrun yours!"

By the time Celeste is finished issuing her dare, Derek,

Jacey, and Doug have already chosen their ostriches and are perched on top with nervous grins.

"There's one more bird, Zoe!" I point to the smallest one. "And she's got the same hairdo as you!"

"Very funny." She climbs on and hugs the bird's neck. "Hey, Mr. Ostrich, beat that kid with the red glasses."

And then we all just . . . sit there, waiting for something to happen.

"How do we get these things to run?" I ask.

Derek puts his fingers to his lips. "You want me to whistle?"

He takes a deep breath, but right before he blows, one of the elephants lifts his trunk and makes a trumpet sound.

The ostriches tear off, thankfully all in the same direction. Jacey's gets the best jump, and she quickly moves into the lead.

"Where are we going?!?" I yell.

"Ha! You finally ask a great question!" Zoe grips the neck of her ostrich as she slips to one side. "Too bad you didn't think to ask *before* we took off!"

Celeste and her bird gallop past me and take the lead from Jacey. She points to an acacia tree a couple hundred feet in the distance. "Let's turn around there!"

"Okay, sure!" I dig my hands in and try to hold on to as many feathers as I can. "I'll just tell my bird, since I speak ostrich!"

"You speak ostrich?" Doug finally catches up to me on the right. "Hey, Arcade, why don't these birds fly?"

"Beats me! That would sure be helpful right now." And

then, my bird slows waaaay down, and everyone passes me! Even Zoe zooms by on the little ostrich.

"See you at the finish, bro! *If* you make it there!" Her pestering laugh rings through the air.

Jacey and Celeste's ostriches are neck and neck as they round the acacia tree. Derek is next, followed by Doug and Zoe. They all reach over to give me high fives as they lap me.

I lean over to talk to my ostrich friend. "Since there are no official rules, let's just turn around here." Another elephant sounds his trumpet, alarming my bird and sending him into a full-on ostrich sprint!

"Duuuuuuuude! HERE WE COME!" I grab hold of his neck and pray I don't end up thrown in the air like I was by Bone Crusher, the bull.

We charge past Zoe, then Doug, then Derek. I can almost feel my bird take flight as we catch Jacey and bear down on Celeste, who is in the lead.

"Oh, no you don't, Arcade!" Celeste yells. "I'm the OSTRICH WHISPERER. You can't beat me!" But as soon as she says that, she falls off the bird's back and disappears in the tall grass! My ostrich and I speed by and take the victory!!

Well, sort of.

"CELESTE! WHERE ARE YOU?" Zoe pulls back on her bird's neck, hops off, and runs to where Celeste disappeared. There's a whole lot of shrieking going on in the grass, so I jump off my bird and go over to see if everyone is all right.

A hand reaches up, grabs my shirt, and pulls me down. I'm face-to-face with Celeste. "You cheated, Arcade. I win."

She's mad and covered in dirt and grass. I'm not arguing with her.

"You got it." I reach out my hand to lift her up. "The winner, by knockoff!"

Celeste dusts off her pants. "You better believe it."

The rest of the gang comes over to check on Celeste.

"Congratulations, Celeste!" Doug says. "Can you guys believe we just raced ostriches in Africa?"

Our friends the ostriches take off toward the acacia tree, leaving us to sit in the tall grass and watch the elephants and giraffes play.

"These animals are stunning." Jacey leans back on her elbows and stares up at the clouds. "There's nothing in the world like them. I wonder why God designed them the way he did?"

I take a moment to study their movements. I imagine trying to race on the back of either a giraffe or an elephant. Nope! Ostriches seem like the best choice for that.

"I don't know, but I'm in awe of them." Zoe nods once. "And speaking of stunning, did you know that Africa has the biggest desert in the world, and the longest river? The Sahara and the Nile." She glances over at me. "Have you ever read that in a book, Arcade?"

"Not yet. But I'll be sure to check one out at the library next time—HEY, ZOE, that reminds me! I have a BLOCK on my library card, and it's YOUR FAULT."

"*My* fault? Oh, no, it couldn't be. I return all my books on time."

I stand up, brush myself off, and put my hands on my hips. "Except for *French Decorating* and *The Care and Feeding of Today's Cockatoo!*"

Zoe looks away. "Uhhhh …"

"Hey, you guys!" Jacey gasps and points to a golden sunset forming in the distance. "Isn't that the prettiest landscape you've seen in your entire life?"

I stop and stare. The sunbeams radiating through the wispy clouds turn into gleaming diamonds that shine on each of my friends' unique faces. I take in a deep breath.

They're each so different. I couldn't have made it this far in my life without them.

"You guys are the best," I say.

"Excuse me, are you children lost?"

We all jump to our feet and turn around. A young man, maybe eighteen, is standing there, making notes on a clipboard.

I thought we were invisible!

He smiles when he sees our faces. "Oh, you are not children. You are teenagers. Welcome to Africa!"

He's wearing dress pants and a short-sleeved dark green shirt with a collar. His wire-framed glasses make him look like some kind of researcher. He's wearing a badge that says "Aahir, Student, Department of Life Sciences."

"Thanks for the welcome. My name is Arcade." I point to his badge. "Is that your name?"

He looks down. "Yes. They make me wear this so

everyone will know I am not a poacher." He narrows his eyes at us. "You are not poachers, are you?"

"Oh, no, we LOVE these animals! We would never think of hurting them." Jacey's smile beams.

He nods. "Oh, good."

"How do you say your name?" Zoe asks.

"Open your mouth and say AH."

We all do it.

"And now, what do your ears help you to do?"

"Hear!" Doug says. "Aahir! That's a great name."

Aahir grins. "It is an Indian name. My mother's ancestors immigrated here to Africa long ago. My father, who is African, liked the name because it means dazzling, brilliant, and to impress deeply."

"Dude! Are you serious?" I grab onto my gold chain.

Aahir looks puzzled. "Well, yes. I am serious about my research."

"No, I mean, is that *really* what your name means?"

He nods. "Yes. That is the meaning. And it fits quite well, since I have always been deeply impressed by the entire world around me! I am out here today as part of a Zoology unit. I am studying these amazing animals. It fascinates me how intricately made they are for the purpose they fulfill. Have you been here long? Have you observed the ostriches? I could watch them all day."

"Up close and personal," Celeste says, and she gives me a smirk as she brushes grass off her elbow.

"Aahir, why don't ostriches fly? It seems like that would be a cool feature."

Especially during a race.

Aahir's eyes light up. "That would be wonderful, wouldn't it? Imagine, you are out on a picnic with your family, and you look up. Is it a giant kite? A small plane? No, it is an ostrich!" He ducks his head and covers it with his clipboard.

We all laugh.

He begins jotting things on his clipboard. "I love imagining the possibilities. But the truth is, the ostrich's physical makeup, with its flat breastbones and small wings, makes it impossible for it to fly. Unless it buys an airplane ticket. Haha!"

I scratch my head. "But it's a bird. Birds fly. Doesn't that drive you nuts not knowing why it's not a *flying* bird?"

Zoe crosses her arms. "My brother likes to ask lots of questions."

Aahir looks up from his clipboard. "It is okay. I love questions! And not knowing something does not bother me at all. I can always study more. Sometimes there is a plausible answer. But when there is not, I am even more in awe!"

"Really? Why?"

"Because sometimes life a mystery, Arcade. A huge, exciting mystery!" He shakes his clipboard in the direction of the ostriches. "We have huge birds on earth that do not fly! How fantastic is that?"

I've never met someone so brilliant who is just as excited about finding things out as he is about *not* finding things out.

"So you're going to be a zoologist?" Derek asks Aahir.

"I do not know. I am interested in ALL the life sciences. That is why I am here at university, to narrow my field.

Or widen it! I will need to read more, study more, and ask questions until I can clearly see what God has in store for me."

"Aahir! The van is leaving!" A girl's voice echoes out over the grassy plain.

Aahir adjusts his glasses. "Oh, dear. I am afraid I must go. It has been wonderful meeting you all."

"Wait!" I say. "I want to talk to you some more. Do you have a card?"

"Card? No, they do not give us cards." He unclips his name badge and hands it to me. "Here you go. Until we meet again."

He runs off to meet his group. And then, two sunbeams flash toward my chest, and the Triple T Token returns to my chain. The beams shoot to the ground, forming a large elevator with antique gold doors below a big sign that says GET TRUTH.

Aahir
Student
Department of Life Sciences

The ride back in the elevator is quiet. We all stare up at the gold-domed ceiling.

Zoe takes her glasses off and squints. "I can almost make out a word on that one." She points to a plaque, then curls her fingers into a loose fist, forming a hole that she peers through. "It pays to be farsighted sometimes." She stares through the hole. "I think it's *enkindleth*. I'm sorry, Arcade. That's all I can see."

"Enkindleth?" Doug laughs. "What kind of word is that?"

Goosebumps pop out all over my arms.

That was on Gertrude's card!

"It's a *great* word. I don't know what it means yet, but it's a golden thread to something profound." I smile at Zoe and reach for my Triple T Token. I look down at the name badge Aahir gave me. "I want to contact Aahir. I could learn a lot from him."

"Good luck with that. You only have his first name, and he's at a university somewhere in *Africa*. Do you know how big Africa is? And we don't even know what year we were just in."

"He said, 'Until we meet again.' It'll happen. I just gotta imagine the possibilities."

And now I have two boys to find!

The elevator doors delivered us back to my living room, where Loopy was licking birthday cake off our plates.

"Loop! I wanted that!" Loopy just looked at me, with his chops full of frosting.

Doug laughed. "Hey, this dog knows what's up." He walked over, picked up the plate, and patted Loopy on the head. "I can cut you another slice, Arcade." He started to go for a plate when my parents came down the stairs with gloves, knit hats, and coats slung over their shoulders.

"Bundle up, gang," Dad said. "It's going to be a windy winter night in New York City!"

The sun sat just above the trees in Central Park, casting a glow on the little mounds of snow that clung to the sides of the walking path we took toward Times Square.

"It would have been quicker to ride the transit, but you

have to see Central Park." Dad hustled our group along the lighted path heading south toward the famous New York City skyscrapers.

"Though you'll never see it all on this trip," said Mom.

"I guess we'll just have to come back. This family seems to have a thing for travel." Jacey turned to look at me as one side of her mouth turned up in a grin.

"Oh, yes," Mom caught up to walk next to Jacey. "Abram and I love to travel. We traveled quite a bit before . . . uh . . . the kids were born."

"Oh, really?" Jacey shot me a knowing glance. "And what was your favorite destination?"

They both answered at the same time. Mom said India. Dad said Africa. It sounded like "Indrica." Then they switched answers, saying them at the same time again. This time, it sounded like "Afria."

"I didn't know you went to those places," Zoe said.

"And we've never seen any pictures," I added.

"And you seem to have pictures of everything else." Zoe narrowed her eyes.

Dad chuckled. "For some reason, whenever your mother and I went on those epic trips, our cameras wouldn't work."

"So we keep the memories alive in here." Mom put her hand on her heart and then looked over at my chest.

Jacey practically knocked me off the trail trying to whisper in my ear. "See? I told you! They know!"

"Where are we going first?" Doug asked. "I hope we're going to Junior's Cheesecake."

"You just spent all day *making* a cake, Doug,"

Doug held his palms to the sky. "But I didn't spend all day *eating* a cake!"

Dad checked his watch. "We thought it would be fun for you kids to see the New York City skyline all lit up from the water, so we booked a harbor cruise. But we have to get there by six-thirty. We'll hail a couple of taxis when we reach the south end of the park."

"It would be quicker to hail an elevator." Doug laughed.

"What?" Mom tilted her head.

"Uh, I meant *operator*. Hail a carriage operator. Or one of those bike guys."

"I'm kinda enjoying just walkin'." Derek took a deep breath. "I've never seen any place like this."

Celeste pushed Derek forward. "Well, walk faster. I'm freezin' and I want to get to the boat."

We picked up the pace as much as we could, with Derek, Celeste, and Jacey gawking at the skyscrapers. When we reached Columbus Circle, Dad flagged down some taxis.

"Pier Sixteen, please," he said to the first taxi driver, and Derek, Doug, Celeste, and Jacey piled into that one. "Zoe and Arcade, you can ride with us." We followed Mom and Dad to the second taxi.

"We haven't had time to give you your present." Mom opened the large tote bag that was sitting on her lap.

"But the surprise *is* my present, right? Did you pay for

everyone's plane tickets? And the cruise . . ." I gestured out the window of the taxi. "You didn't have to get me a gift too."

Mom reached into the tote. "It's not anything big, really. Just something that we thought would be meaningful to you." She pulled out a plain cardboard box that was all taped up.

"You've been carrying this through the park? It's kinda heavy."

"Ha! Have you ever felt my purse? I'm a strong woman."

"I agree." I pulled the first little bag out of the box. I peeked in and laughed. "Library card socks!" They were yellow, with a pattern like the old cards that used to be in the pocket of library books before everything went tech. "I'm wearing these on Friday."

I wear crazy socks on Fridays. The rest of the days, well . . . I don't wear socks.

"That's not all there is." Dad took the socks from me and leaned forward.

I sat the box on the floor of the cab and dug in with both hands, pulling out a heavy ball of tissue paper taped around an odd-shaped item. I started to rip.

Zoe sighed. "Hurry up, Arcade."

I tried to hurry up, but for each sheet of tissue paper I pulled off, there was one underneath. "I'm surprised you're giving me something breakable." I laughed and kept peeling the paper away. When I finally unwrapped it all, I held a pair of bookends in my lap! When they were pressed together, they formed a domed building with a little torch on top.

"This is cool. I don't have any bookends."

Mom shifted her eyes to Dad, and then smiled at me.

"Well, for someone who loves books so much, it's about time you got some."

"Thanks, guys. They're perfect. I'll put all my favorites in these."

"That would be appropriate, considering—"

"Pier Sixteen!" the cab driver yelled. Then he gazed out his driver's side window. "Not a cloud in the sky. You're a brave bunch for taking a winter cruise. Even Lady Liberty will be shivering tonight."

I carefully rewrapped the bookends and handed them to Mom so she could store them in her tote. I pulled on my hoodie *and* my heavy jacket, and then followed my family and friends to Pier Sixteen.

When we cruised by the Statue of Liberty, Dad put his hand on my shoulder. "I'm sorry we haven't had much time to tour New York City with you, Arcade. Life's been so busy. I hope this makes up for it a little." He pointed up, way up, to the top of the majestic statue. "One time your mom and I went all the way to the crown. I'm sure we'll get a chance to take you there soon."

I grinned.

I've already been there.

We got off the cruise around nine o'clock. Thankfully, New York City was just getting started for the night. We ice skated at Rockefeller Center, buzzed through Times Square, took selfies in front of St. Peter's Cathedral, and ate s'mores at the Hershey store. And, of course, Doug got a piece of strawberry cheesecake at Junior's.

Celeste, Derek, Jacey, Zoe, and I all bought matching *I Love New York* beanies from a cool guy with a street cart. And yes, you better believe we filled ourselves up with hot dogs, pretzels, and roasted chestnuts too.

"Where to next?" Doug spoke through a mouthful of pretzel.

"It's two a.m.!" Zoe rubbed her eyes. "Some of us need our beauty sleep." She dragged herself up Broadway, where we took more selfies next to all the theater marquees. "Do we *have* to walk all the way to 88th?"

"NO, we don't." Mom was limping just a little on one side. "I'm calling us some rides. We have to save *some* energy for tomorrow."

Doug came over and poked me with his elbow. "It would be cool if your elevators would take us home. Or get us back to those ostriches. I want a rematch."

I reached for my token, which was hidden under all my layers. "Yeah, and I'd like to talk to Aahir again. But it's best if Triple T stays calm for now."

Sunday was a blur. We hailed taxis, caught the subway, rode buses, and took about a thousand pictures of ourselves all over Manhattan. For lunch, we popped into Brooklyn for some famous New York-style pizza. Then we walked back over the Brooklyn Bridge.

Doug dropped behind, holding onto the railing near the walkway. "Arcade, I'm sweatin' and it's forty degrees out. When we gonna get off this bridge?"

Jacey turned and pointed to the New York skyline. "Arcade, we *have* to get a picture together with that in the background!"

Zoe ribbed me with her elbow. "Yes, you absolutely must. Give me your phone, I'll take a photo of you two. Together. You're such a cute couple."

"Stop it, Zoe. We're NOT a couple."

"But she came all the way from Virginia."

"To see New York City."

"To see *you*. Arcade, don't be a numb-brain! She's a nice girl."

"Can you just take the picture, please?"

Zoe grinned. "Okay, hand over the phone."

I ran over to Jacey.

Where should I stand? Don't get too close.

Before I could figure out what to do, Jacey threw her arm over my shoulder and pulled me in!

"Say 'cheesecake!'" Doug yelled from the rail.

"Cheesecake!" Jacey shouted, but I was speechless. Zoe snapped a dozen pictures of us, close ups, further backs,

more of the skyline, more of us. And in all of them, my
expression was the same—confused and freaked out.

"Can we take a carriage ride in the park?" Jacey was bubblier
than usual in the afternoon. Everyone else was just tired.

"Anything that will get us off our feet." Zoe fell back
behind everybody.

Thankfully, we didn't have to endure the "romantic"
carriage ride, because we ran into our favorite pedicab tour
guide, Elijah. He was standing in Columbus Circle with all
the other bike tour guides, all bundled up for the cold, trying
to drum up business.

"Arcade! Zoe! It is so nice to see you. What are you
doing out here today? It is a bit brisk!"

"How's business, Elijah?" Zoe gathered our whole group
around our friend from Senegal.

He shook his head. "Not so good. Who are all these
friends?"

"You know me!" Doug emerged from the back of the
pack, munching on some warm chestnuts.

"Oh, yes, my food-loving brother. How did it work out
with your grandmother? Are you living with her still?"

Doug licked his fingers. "No, she's in a special care place
in the city. I live with Arcade now."

Elijah clapped his hands together. "Oh, what a blessing!"

"Hello, friend." My dad reached out his hand to shake

Elijah's. "I would like to hire you to take us on a quick tour of the park. These kids are due back at the airport soon."

Elijah's eyes widened. "I am afraid my bike will only fit three people. But I have a couple other tour guide friends who would like some work today."

My dad grinned. "Well, bring them over! Arcade, Doug, and Derek can ride with you, Celeste, Zoe, and Jacey can ride in another, and Dottie and I will ride together."

"That is wonderful," Elijah said. "I will be right back."

As we waited for Elijah to return with more tour guides, Celeste pulled me and Zoe aside. "I want to ride with Doug."

I rolled my eyes. "Really, Celeste? He's two years younger than you."

"I don't care. He's fun and he's cute, and I want to hear his Central Park commentary."

"It's no trouble, Celeste," Zoe said. "Arcade will switch with you. He's kind and understanding like that." She reached over and yanked the top of my beanie. "Right, bro?"

Elijah returned with two bundled-up guys with pedicabs. "Okay, friends, hop in for the express tour. I can ride fast to keep warm. But you will all have to snuggle up."

My heart started to pound. "Uh, you mean bundle up, right, Elijah?"

He laughed. "Whatever works for you, my friend."

We all hopped into the bike taxis. I ended up squashed between Zoe and Jacey. I had no plans to snuggle up.

When we finally arrived home, we barely had time to get everyone's suitcases in the car. And since our car wouldn't hold us all, Zoe, Doug, and I had to say goodbye at the house before the rest of them drove off to the airport.

"Best day I've had in a long time. When you movin' back to Virginia?" Derek popped his backward visor on his head and gave me a fist bump and a hug.

"Not soon enough. Maybe I'll go to college out there."

Derek sighed. "Okay. Well, don't be a stranger." He bumped my token with his knuckle and whispered. "Maybe this'll bring you out."

"You never know."

"See ya, Arcade." Celeste punched me in the arm. "Happy birthday."

I gave her a side hug. "Thanks, Celeste."

Jacey approached with tears in her eyes. "Thank you for a wonderful time." She gave me a big hug.

"You're welcome." I stepped back and said something else, but I can't remember what.

And then they were gone.

CHAPTER 10
Tired Morning

ometimes it's a good thing that our homeroom teacher, Mr. Dooley, has a loud voice. Especially when you're struggling to stay awake on Monday morning.

"AHEM . . . NEW ASSIGNMENT! TIME TRAVEL. IS IT POSSIBLE? WRITE IT UP. THREE PAGES. WHAT DO YOU KNOW ABOUT SCIENCE THAT COULD LEAD YOU TO BELIEVE IN TIME TRAVEL? CONVINCE ME, PEOPLE!"

I sat up a little straighter and pinched myself.

Did Mr. Dooley just ask us to write about time travel? Or am I just dreaming?!?

"Hey, Arcade, you got any paper? I'm out." My friend Carlos James "CJ" Mendoza patted me on the arm. I sit next to him in the back row of the classroom. It's the only place he can fit with his wheelchair.

"Uh, yeah, sure Carlos. I have lots." I reached into my flamingo backpack, pulled out my notebook, and unlatched the three rings to get a few sheets of paper out. "Did Mr. Dooley just ask about time travel?"

Carlos chuckled. "Yeah. He wants us to use our imagination mixed with some evidence." Carlos leaned in close. "Should we write about your token? It did take us back three years."

Carlos was with us in the crown of the Statue of Liberty when we were looking for Loopy. The token took us back in time, before Carlos's car accident, when he could walk. It was dope!

"I think we better keep that a secret. But, hey! Check this out. If I got on a plane right now and flew to California, it would be three hours earlier than here, so there's your answer. We *can* time travel."

Doug, who sits by me on my other side, chimed in. "And if we somehow kept traveling west, past the earth somehow, could we *keep* going back in time? Is that how we got to the pyramids when they were building them?"

"You guys went to the pyramids? You gotta tell me about that some time." Carlos wheeled himself a little closer to my desk.

Doug continued, "And then, if we go *east* and spin off the globe, could we fly into the *future*, like the time I was a grown-up pastry chef on *The Munch*? Arcade, do you think there's another dimension we haven't considered here? Is that how the token works?"

"YOUNG MEN IN THE BACK ROW, THIS IS NOT A COMMITTEE PROJECT."

I folded my hands on the desk. "Uh, sorry, Mr. Dooley. We were just . . . imagining possibilities."

"Well, for this project, imagine them all on your own,

and don't speak about it. WRITE IT DOWN." He walked back behind his desk, sat down, and grinned. "I give such fun assignments."

I pulled out my own sheet of paper and tapped my pen on the desk.

Time travel . . . hmmm. Is that how the token works? Is that why Ruah is young and then she's old? Is that why my age sometimes changes when we go through the elevator doors? Is that why I was able to leave the Badger brothers in 1935 . . . and then bring them back? Where are those brothers right now?

I uncapped the pen and wrote my title:

Time Travel . . . It Is Possible!
By Arcade Livingston

Then I wrote my opening sentence:

I believe that time travel is possible. We just haven't figured out how to do it yet. Here are the truths I know about this . . .

I've been doing it. And I really need to get back to Greece!

CHAPTER 11

Volleyball
Villain

I barely made it through the day. The only time I had a small surge of energy was during lunch, so I jetted to the school library to check out books about Greece, only to find out they didn't have any!

"Why not? Who checked them out?"

The student helper, a tall girl with a huge, messy bun on top of her head, scanned the computer screen. "Looks like an eighth grader checked them out a month ago, but he returned them soaking wet. We had to damage them out, and we haven't purchased replacements yet."

"WET? That's horrifying! Who gets library books wet? Don't they know that books are IMPORTANT?"

The girl held up her hands. "Hey, I agree! And I feel your pain. I love books, or I wouldn't work here." She gave me a sympathetic glance and scanned the computer again. "Are you interested in travel? We have plenty of books on Italy, Spain, and Australia."

I held my head in my hands. "Noooo. I NEED Greece."

She turned from the screen and tapped her fingers on

the counter. "Sorry. I guess you'll have to check the public library."

"I did. I have a block on my card."

"A BLOCK? What did *you* do? Turn in wet books?"

"NO! I have a sister who abused my generous nature."

"Oh, dear. I'm so sorry . . . uh . . ." she checked my name on the computer. "Arcade? That's your name? Did you know that an arcade is a part of the architecture of ancient Greece?"

"Yes, I'm aware of that! That's one of the reasons I'm trying to check out books about Greece."

She put her hand to her mouth. "Oh. Now it all makes sense. I'm so sorry."

"No problem. You did all you could."

I made my way to the last exhausting class of the day—PE. I forced myself into my workout clothes, dragged myself to the gym, and came face-to-face with a bunch of . . . girls!

"Hey, Arcade! Today we're playin' girls! Think you could do something athletic for a change so we don't look so bad?" Casey Tolley gave me a little push. "Hehe, just kiddin', buddy. Let's kick 'em to the curb. I'll try not to trip you."

Just what I need—a humiliation tournament.

I barely had the energy to walk to the gym, let alone play at the top of my game against a bunch of girls *and* watch out for Casey Tolley's foot.

"All right, gentlemen, it's time to play our best female teams in the school. Be alert, these girls can spike!"

Spike?

Our PE teacher, Mr. Bell, stood on the sidelines of the gym. He checked his watch. "We'll have both courts running. Each game is fifteen minutes, the winner plays the next team till the end of the period. The last team standing is the winner." He pulled a whistle up to his mouth. "Okay, take your positions. Mr. Livingston, what side of this court are you on?"

I was zoning out and didn't realize I was on the wrong side of the net. The *girls'* side! I did my best to keep my cool, duck under the net without clotheslining myself, and grabbed the position in the front row, middle. On the *boys'* side.

"GAME ON!" Mr. Bell announced, and blew his whistle.

Girls served first, and the short girl in the back row missed.

Okay, this is what I'm talking about!

"Serve, boys!"

My big "friend," Wiley Overton, whose hands made the volleyball look more like a softball, smacked it over, sending it rocketing toward the back row at the girl who had missed the serve. She stuck her fist up, got a piece of it, but sent it flying out of bounds into the bleachers.

"It's okay, Paris, good try!" a tall, athletic-looking girl with long brown hair in the front row yelled out. Then she turned and pointed right at me. "We're just getting warmed up." Her eyes flickered with energy.

I'd like to borrow some of that right now.

Wiley got the ball again and slugged it like a beast. It

went sailing toward Paris again, who backed up, just as the girl from the front row dove for it and bumped it into play!

Whoa, she's good.

A tall, redheaded girl moved into the center of the court and executed the perfect set. The ball flew up in the air, just high enough for Athletic Girl to get up off the floor and move back to her position. The ball came down just in front her, a few inches above the net. She jumped up, opened her hand, and spiked the ball. I jumped up . . . and returned it!

With my face.

Phhhhttttttttt!

Mr. Bell's whistle echoed through the gym and inside my head. At least I thought I still had my head. I reached up to check.

"Livingston! You alright?" All I knew was that I was on the floor, and I couldn't see anything. I put my hand up to feel blood coming out of my nose. My glasses were gone.

"Arcade?" Casey Tolley's voice sounded in my ear. "You need us to call 9-1-1? Dude, you face-spiked it!"

"Way to go, Arcade," Wiley said. "You got us the point!"

Mr. Bell handed me a rag to catch the flow from my nose.

"GET OUT OF THE WAY, PEOPLE! Can't you see he's bleeding?" Through my blurred vision, I could see Athletic Girl pushing boys out of the way so she could get to me.

"Are you okay? I'm so sorry! I didn't mean to hit you in the face!" She began barking orders. "Someone get him some WATER! And WHERE are his glasses?" She looked at me. "You *were* wearing glasses, right?"

I nodded. "Mmm-hmmm."

"I got 'em," Casey yelled. "They're over here. Oh, wait, they're over here too."

That doesn't sound good.

Casey came running over and handed Athletic Girl two pieces of my glasses. She gave them to me and frowned sympathetically. "I am SOOO sorry."

"We're losing time, people. We've got a tournament going here. Let's

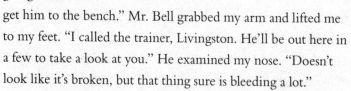

get him to the bench." Mr. Bell grabbed my arm and lifted me to my feet. "I called the trainer, Livingston. He'll be out here in a few to take a look at you." He examined my nose. "Doesn't look like it's broken, but that thing sure is bleeding a lot."

Athletic Girl put a hand up to her mouth. "It's my fault, Mr. Bell. I don't think I can continue until I know he's going to be okay."

"Get out there, Elena. Livingston will be fine. It was *his* fault for not blocking with his hands."

"But—" She looked like she was going to cry.

Mr. Bell pointed to the court. "Get back in the game, Castro!"

The girl gave me another sympathetic glance and

dropped her chin. "Yes, sir," she said quietly, and ran back to her position.

I balanced my broken glasses frames on top of my nose and watched the game as best I could until the trainer got there. The girls took the lead when Elena finally got to the serving position. That girl could do a running overhand spike serve!

Why didn't I block with my hands?

Elena was right in the middle of every single play that followed—digging, setting, or spiking the ball over the net for a point.

Well, at least I got injured by the best.

Mr. Lozano, the trainer, finally arrived and sat next to me. "You got hands, Mr. Livingston? That's what most people use to block the ball." He removed the rag from my nose. "Bleeding's stopped. That's good." He shined a stick light into both of my eyes. "Responsive, good." Then he tilted his head both ways and pushed his fingers on the sides of my nose. "That hurt?"

"No, sir."

He pulled his hands back and patted me on the shoulder. "Looks like the only thing broken are your glasses." He held his hand out and I placed the two pieces into his palm. "Broke clean right here on the nosepiece. I got tape for that." He pulled some white therapy tape from of his fanny pack and cut a thin piece with medical scissors. He wrapped it around the nosepiece. "There. Good as new."

Awesome.

"You want me to call your parents to give you a ride home today? That was a pretty good shot to the face."

"Nah. I can walk home."

He looked closer into my eyes. "You sure?"

"Yep."

"Okay. I'm gonna give them a call though. Might be good to let the doc take a look, just to make sure your nose isn't broken. You don't want to end up with a deviated septum or something awful like that." He smacked me on the other arm. "And I'd stay far away from the person who did that to you." He laughed.

Phhhhtttttttt!

"First game goes to the girls! Boys, team two, you're in!"

I glanced over at the girls' team that had just annihilated us. They were high-fiving each other. All except Elena. She was looking over my way, waving, and mouthing the words . . .

"I'M SO SORRY."

CHAPTER 12
Elena Salva-DOR Castro

Doug met me out in front of the school for our regular walk home through Central Park.

"What happened to your glasses?"

"I spiked a volleyball."

Doug reached up as if he were going to hit a volleyball. "So . . . what happened to your glasses?"

"I did it with my face."

Doug grabbed his chest and pretended he was falling backward. "Duuuude, that's rough! What you need is a snack. Lucky we still got tons of birthday cake left."

"It seems like my birthday was days ago." I started moving toward the trail.

Doug walked next to me, his hand on my shoulder. "That's how things are here in New York City. We cram a lot into both days and nights. Hey! I still have to give you my present."

"A present? Doug, the cake was amazing. You didn't have to get me a present."

"Oh, yes I did! Wait till you see—"

"EXCUSE ME! ARCADE! IS THAT YOU?"

A nervous knot formed in my stomach. It sounded a lot like the volleyball villain Mr. Lozano told me to stay away from.

"C'mon, Doug." I tightened my backpack straps and picked up the pace.

"Arcaaaade! Wait up, please! I have something for you."

"Pretend you don't hear that," I whispered.

Doug jogged alongside me. "But I *do* hear it, and she's gaining on us. Don't you think we should stop? She sounds like she really wants to talk to you."

"But I don't want to talk to her."

"Why not?"

"ARCAAAADE!" I felt a strong tug on the loop on the top of my backpack. So strong, I lost my balance and fell on my backside.

"Oh, NO! I'm so sorry. I didn't mean—"

Elena reached out to help me up, but I hopped up on my own, dusting my hands off.

"So, you here to finish me off?"

"No! I came to apologize."

Doug stuck a hand out. "Doug Baker, Arcade's best friend and soon-to-be brother. Who are you and why are you sweeping my friend off his feet?"

Elena didn't take her eyes off me. "Elena Salvador Castro." She reached out and pointed to the tape on my glasses. "Do you have a back-up pair?"

I pushed my glasses up on my nose. "No."

Elena sighed. "I was afraid of that. I want to pay for a new pair of glasses."

"That's not necessary." I began walking. *Fast*. But Elena kept up.

"No, you don't understand. I want to be an eye doctor someday! Well, either that, or a missionary. Or, I've been thinking of mixing the two—"

I stopped. Elena flew by and had to back up.

"Wait, you know what you want to be when you grow up? That's a hard thing to figure out."

"You better believe it!" Doug added. "You should have been there last year when we were trying to figure that out for the career expo! So far, all I know is that I'm working with food."

Elena still wouldn't take her eyes off my glasses. "I'm not going to feel better unless you let me buy you some new glasses." She reached into her athletic bag and pulled out a pad of sticky notes. Then she took out a pen and scribbled something on it. "Here. This is my phone number, and the other number is our house phone. Call me, or you can have your parents call. I'll pay for your glasses."

I just stared at her. "That's not necessary. It's my fault for blocking with my face."

She held out the note. I didn't reach out to grab it. She tried to stick it on my arm, but I stepped back. She tried to stick it to my backpack strap, but I dodged. She attempted to hand it to Doug, but he just threw his hands up. "Aw, no, I'm not gettin' in the middle of this!"

Elena crunched her eyebrows together and tilted her head to the side. "You're a funny kid, Livingston. Why won't you let me help you?"

I could tell she had a good heart, but my pride was at stake here.

She stuck the note on my sweaty forehead. "Call me."

The note fell off and fluttered to the ground. I left it there and started walking.

"Litterbug!" Elena called after me.

I walked faster. Doug came up alongside. "Man, I never knew you were so stubborn. Why didn't you just take the note? You don't have to call."

"Can we change the subject? It's been a long, awful day. And now I have to go to the doctor to make sure I don't have a deviated septum."

"Deviated septum? Sounds gnarly. What's that?"

"I have no idea. I'd check a book out about it, but I also have a *blocked library card*."

Doug nodded. "So *that's* it! That's why you're so grouchy!"

I glanced over at Doug, annoyed at the way this whole afternoon had turned out. "Let's change the subject. How was the rest of *your* day, Doug?"

Doug looked back over his shoulder. "It . . . was . . . I got a disturbing . . . call . . . um, Arcade, that girl is following us."

"What girl?" I asked, knowing *exactly* what girl he was talking about. I refused to look.

"Elena Salvatore Castro."

"You mean, Elena Salva-DOR Castro?"

"Yeah. That one."

"Let's get out of the park." We took the exit from Central Park on 90th and crossed the street.

"She still there?" I whispered to Doug.

"Yeeeah."

"I'VE GOT ALL DAY, LIVINGSTON!"

Doug threw his head back and laughed. "This is ridiculous. Can't you just take the note?"

"NO."

"No?"

"No."

"Why not?"

"Because I just want to forget about it and her."

"I'M GOING TO FOLLOW YOU ALL THE WAY HOME, LIVINGSTON!"

Doug laughed again. "Okay, well, good luck with that. Whatcha gonna do, man?"

I picked up my pace. "I don't know. She's more stubborn than Zoe, and I didn't think that was possible."

Thankfully Zoe wasn't meeting us on the way home today. She was going somewhere with Michael Tolley. I'd never live this down if she were here.

"You gonna let her follow us *all the way*?" By now, Doug was huffing and puffing, jogging next to me. "She looks like she could outrun us both."

"That's the truth, Doug. We're gonna have to duck through an alley and try to lose her." I picked up the pace. "Hey, let's take that one." I pointed to a shortcut that Zoe and I sometimes use to get to the subway station. We rounded the turn into the narrow, dark alley.

Just as we did, Triple T came to life, shining stars of light on the sidewalk and buildings around us!

"That's some blinding stuff!" Doug shielded his eyes with his forearm. "What happened to all the glitter? And the fire?"

"I don't know. It's been doing this new light thing lately. Just hang with me, Doug. I think we're going someplace. Someplace Elena Salvador Castro can't follow."

I pulled my token out of my shirt and the rays of light hit the sidewalk, forming a golden elevator.

Doug shook his head in disbelief. "Every time this happens, it blows me away!"

We watched as a sign that said GET TRUTH rose from the ground in front of the elevator doors, and a coin slot appeared right below it.

"Hey, guys, wait up!"

I almost jumped out of my shirt when I realized who it was. *Zoe*. With Michael Tolley!

Noooo!

"Thought you'd make it all the way home without your big sis?" Zoe's eyes popped when she saw the elevator. "Oh, no . . ."

"What IS this?" Michael moved in closer, touching the sign and then the coin slot. I expected him to freak out, like most people do when they first see the elevator. But Michael kept inspecting everything. "Wow! What will New York City think of next?" He walked around the elevator, and then he spotted my token, pulsing light toward the coin slot.

He pointed. "What is THAT?"

Zoe said, "That's, uh, a little hard to explain."

"It's a family secret." Doug crossed his arms and leaned

against the elevator. "Only a few people know about it. You can't tell anybody. Especially Kevin and Casey."

Michael smiled. "I love secrets. What does it do?"

"That . . . is . . . also hard to explain," Zoe said.

"You gotta just go with it." Doug approached the doors.

"*Go* with it?" Michael inspected the elevator again. "Is there a way to get inside?"

"Oh, yeah." I turned to Zoe and raised my eyebrows.

Should I?

She glanced over at Michael, and then back at me before raising her palms in the air. "Do we have any choice?"

"ARCADE LIVINGSTON! WAIT UP!"

Elena.

"We gotta go. NOW!" I pulled the token from the chain, stepped up to the coin slot, and stared into the GET TRUTH sign.

"Give me an -est. A WIDE-est!"

Anything to get me away from the Volleyball Villain!

I dropped the token in the slot, and immediately made an open-door motion with my hands. The ancient golden doors slowly rolled open.

"Come on!" I shoved everybody in. "CLOSE!"

Once again, they rolled. Slowly.

Sweat streamed down my back, even though it was thirty degrees outside. I took off my glasses to wipe the fog away.

Zoe pointed to the tape in the middle. "What happened? You get hit in the face?"

"NO. I hit something with my face."

"That's the same thing."

"No, it's not."

"Yes, it is."

Okay, maybe she is more stubborn than Elena. Either way, I only need one of them in my life.

"Check THAT out!" Michael stared up at the gold-domed ceiling. "Where are we going? Rome? London? This ceiling reminds me of St. Paul's Cathedral."

"Is it wide in London?" I asked.

"Wide?" Michael gave me a puzzled look.

"Because we're going someplace wide," Zoe said.

The elevator creaked and jolted. Michael squinted toward the dome. "Wish I could read those plaques."

"Me too." I adjusted my glasses to see if it would help.

Nope.

Maybe I should let Elena buy me some new glasses.

Nope.

As soon as the elevator doors open, I feel like I've been wrapped in a hot, wet blanket.

There's wood under my feet. It's creaky, like the elevator, and it's rocking a bit, like the elevator.

But it's not an elevator.

"Canoes! I HATE canoes!" Zoe has hated canoes ever since that one summer when we rented one on the James River, and I purposely rocked it to tip us over. I was surprised how hard it was to get it turned *back* over. We had to flag down a boat to save us, which took over an hour.

"Better grab some paddles and stay in the middle so we don't tip." Although he's never been on an Arcade adventure before, Michael is the calm voice of reason. "Where do you think we are, Zoe?"

There are three benches inside the canoe. Michael takes the one in the back, Zoe sits on the one in front of him, and Doug and I have to squeeze in together on the one in the front. We're all wearing gold life vests over our coats, which make us pretty thick.

Monkeys squeal and swing from trees on the shore.

"Zoe, you think this is a rain forest?" As soon as I say that, I get my answer. It begins to rain. *Hard.*

"YES! I think it's the AMAZON rain forest, and thanks a LOT, Arcade! Now I'm hot and DRENCHED!" Zoe dips her paddle in the water and sends a wave over my head.

Too bad we're not wearing our *waterproof* winter coats.

"Where we paddlin' to?" Doug spits rain from his mouth.

Then I spot it. It's a glowing message, carved into the wood at the front of the canoe.

DESTINATION: OTHER SIDE. APPROX. TWENTY-FOUR MILES.

"Uh, guys? The sign says we're going to the other side of this . . . is this a river or a lake? Because it's twenty-four miles to the other side."

"That's wide!" Doug shouts. "Must be a huge lake."

"Everybody, pull your paddles out of the water." Michael's commands are firm. We do as he tells us. But the canoe keeps moving with the current of the . . .

"It's the Amazon RIVER!" Zoe squeals. "It has to be! We're in a CANOE on the AMAZON RIVER!"

That jogs a fact from my brain. "That's right! I've read that the Amazon is the world's widest river."

"You read too much!" Zoe pokes me with her paddle.

"That's not possible! Plus, it helps, because now I know why the token brought us here."

"Why would you ask it to bring us to a *wide* place?"

"He just wanted to get far away from Elena Salvatore Castro." Doug picks up his paddle to splash me. Like a few more drops are going to get me any wetter than I already am.

"Salva-DOR! It's Salva-DOR!" I yell through the rain as we paddle and paddle.

"Who's Elena Salvador Castro?" Zoe pokes me again.

"She's the girl who hit Arcade in the face with a volley-ball," Doug yells.

"She didn't hit me in the face." I dig my paddle in harder.

"Ooooooh," Zoe says. "So that's how your glasses got broken. The truth always comes out."

The mighty Amazon current picks up. Soon we're no longer paddling across the river, but being pulled *down* it.

"Paddle harder, team!" Michael commands. "We have to turn so we can get to the shore."

Doug holds his hand above his eyes. "What shore? I can't see a shore."

"It's there," I say. "But it might as well be a million miles away."

"Who makes a river *this* wide?" Doug continues to search the area for land.

"God does!" Michael yells from the back.

"Yes," I say, "but for what purpose?"

Why is the Amazon River an -EST?

"To hold ALL THE RAIN!" Zoe splashes me again. "Now, PADDLE, ARCADE, OR ELSE!"

I push my paddle in the water and give it a strong pull, which jerks the canoe to the right. I stand and turn around to talk to Zoe. "There! Are you happy?" The sight of my sister totally drenched in her winter coat and life vest makes me laugh. And then I slip, lose my footing, and fall against Doug.

"HEY!" Doug catches me, and now he's laughing too.

The canoe dips hard to one side.

And when canoes do that, they tip over.

The water in the Amazon River is warm, just like the air. And it's wet, like the air. I'm thankful for the life vests.

I feel myself being pulled by the river current, so I grab the tipped canoe and hold on.

"Zoe! Michael! Doug!" I scream but get choked by a wave of warm water that splashes into my mouth.

"ARCADE! I'm over here!" I spot Doug, hanging onto the front of the tipped canoe.

"Here!" Michael yells. I turn back and can barely see his hand as he waves it above the back of the canoe.

"Guys! Where's Zoe?"

Oh, no. I'm so sorry, Zoe. I was just having a little fun.

"ZOE!" I yell at the top of my lungs.

Nothing.

I let go of the canoe and swim hard upstream to try to find her. It's no use. The mighty Amazon pulls me downstream, and all I find is the canoe.

"Arcade!" Michael shouts. "Stay with the canoe! I'll find her!"

"ZOE!" I yell again, feeling helpless.

And then I see it. A gold bump, stuck in a . . . tree?

How is a tree in the middle of a river?

I can't see her face. I can only pray she's not stuck under water. I swim as hard as I can, but Michael is a stronger swimmer and reaches her first.

"Arcade!" Zoe cries. "Over here! I'm over here."

I paddle and kick as hard as I can. As I get closer, I see that her hair is caught in the tree branches, and she and Michael are desperately trying to work her free.

"Hang on, Zoe, I'm coming!" I can't see the canoe anymore. Doug will have to fend for himself. The rain pounds down so hard that I can't tell where it ends and where the river begins. I choke, I swim, and, somehow, my broken glasses stay on my face.

Finally, I reach the tree and grab onto some branches near Zoe.

"Zoe, I'm so sorry, I didn't mean to tip the canoe."

"I know. Just get me out of here."

"Okay." I'm smaller than Michael, so I'm able to squeeze between the branches and pull myself up to the place where Zoe's hair tie is caught.

"You should think about a different hairstyle from now on." I grab on to the tie and pull.

"Very funn—OUCH! Just cut me loose!"

"What am I supposed to cut it with?"

"Here."

Michael climbs within an arm's length of me and hands me a pocketknife.

"Whoa, that's convenient!"

When we get home, I'm getting one of these.

I wedge myself in between the branches and use both hands to open the knife. Then I grab back on and pull myself closer to Zoe.

"Hurry, Arcade!"

The river has risen. The water is now up to Zoe's chin. Small waves roll over her head. I grip her ponytail . . .

And the knife slips out of my hand!

"NOOOOOO!"

"Did you get it, Arcade?" Zoe spits and chokes, and the next wave totally covers her face.

"Zoe, hang on, I've almost got it."

What I don't tell her or Michael is that the knife is now downstream somewhere with Doug and the canoe.

Help me, God. This is a huge river, but I know you see us.

I grab the hair tie with both hands and tug in opposite directions, hoping I can snap it. It happens to Zoe all the time when she's not even trying! This must be a new one, though, because I can hardly stretch it.

Come on, token. The testing is over. I'm supposed to be getting truth here!

"Arcade, cut the tie! You can do it!" Michael is holding onto Zoe, trying to keep her head out of the river.

He's one of the good guys. That's the truth.

And then, my life vest begins to glow.

I keep hold of the branch with one hand and, with the other, I reach through the vest, under my coat, and find it. The Triple T Token. Hanging on the end of my chain.

"Back from the mold! It's about time!"

I pull it off.

Do NOT drop it, Arcade!

It feels sticky in my hand, and it shoots out a laser, straight toward Zoe's hair. It cuts a hunk off the end of her ponytail.

"Oops!"

"What do you mean, *oops*?" Zoe's head is above water now.

I decide this isn't the time to tell her she won't be needing a haircut for a while.

I aim the laser at Zoe's hair tie. It slices it with ease.

"I got it, Zoe! I got it!"

"Yes!" Michael punches his fist in the water.

"Good job, little bro! I knew you could do it!"

Zoe, Michael, and I keep holding the branches so we aren't pulled downstream. Zoe looks around. "Where's Doug?"

"DOUG!" All three of us yell at the same time.

"Over here! By the shore!" Doug shouts even louder than the roar of the river.

Zoe, Michael, and I swim as fast as we can toward Doug. The river's current is strong, but we're stronger, desperate to reach our friend. I can see the wooden canoe laying on its side on the shore next to a golden elevator and coin slot. Doug is thrashing around in the water.

"Doug, we gotta get to the elevator. Is your foot stuck in a branch?"

Doug yelps, "Yeah, if a branch has teeth!"

Teeth?

Suddenly, I wish I had never read that library book about river monsters.

Michael pulls himself out of the water. "Zoe, get up on shore. Arcade and I will help Doug."

"It's got my foot in its mouth." Doug winces. "But I must not taste good 'cause he hasn't bit it off yet."

I still have the Triple T laser token clenched in my hand. I keep one eye on Doug and another on the coin slot.

Hang on, elevator. I can't leave here without Doug.

Doug manages to pull most of his body up on the shore. His legs are still in the water. He reaches in and feels around. "I think it's a catfish. It has a big, flat head and whiskers!"

I see a tail flick out of the water about ten feet from where Doug has his foot caught.

Zoe screams. "Th . . . th . . . that's the biggest catfish I've *ever* seen!"

I scramble out of the water onto shore. "It's a river monster! Everybody, stand back!"

I hold up the token, and the laser shoots a thin black tunnel through the mud in front of me as I run toward Doug.

"You gonna cut my foot off, Arcade?" Doug's eyes are as wide as dinner plates.

"NO! I'm just going to give him a little headache."

"And make him SO MAD he'll bite my foot off?"

I stop. The laser continues to zap a hole in the mud near my feet. "Hmmm. Never thought of that." I scratch my head. "Gotta rethink this."

"No time, Arcade!" Zoe points to the coin slot, which is starting to fade away.

What truth do I know about catfish? They're bottom-feeders!

"Make him go to the bottom of the river!" I shout.

The laser coming out of the token changes to dazzling light. I know what to do. I squat next to Doug.

"I got you, bro. Pull your foot up so I can see its eyes."

Doug grunts and struggles before forcing his leg slightly out of the water. I almost faint when I see the huge thing. I point the token at its eyes . . . and pray. It does the trick. The river monster jerks back, opens its mouth, and sinks out of sight.

"Arcade, the elevator is disappearing!" Zoe grabs the back of my life vest and pulls me toward the coin slot. "Throw it in! Hurry!"

I glance back at Doug. "You good?"

He jumps up on the one, non-chewed foot. "Oh, yeah. You're not gettin' rid of me that easy. I know you want my top bunk," he laughs, hobbling toward the antique doors.

Michael walks shoulder to shoulder next to Zoe. "Does this happen often? Cause if it does, I'll pass next time."

Zoe smiles and grabs her hair to wring it out. And then she realizes the truth.

"Arcade! What did you do?"

"Uh, Zoe, about your hair . . ." I throw the token in the

slot and make the open-door motion with my hands. "It's a new technique. A laser cut. You're going to start a new fad. You'll see."

And with that, I step in and say another prayer. This time, that my sister doesn't tackle me.

We stand in the elevator, dripping.

"That was the scariest moment of my life." Zoe unbuckles her life vest and throws it to the floor. "Why in the world did you ask the token to take us somewhere wide? Surely not just to get away from some girl."

"Ruah said something about wide, long, high, and deep. I figured there was some truth in wide."

Michael Tolley pulls off his life vest and gawks at the gold ceiling again. "And did you find some?"

"Yeah, I did. I found out that you're a pretty cool dude." I trace my index finger in a circle around my token and then extend my hand. "We cool with this?"

Michael grins and shakes my hand. "Oh, yeah. I won't tell anyone. Especially my brothers."

I blow out a breath. "Thanks."

CHAPTER 14

Bottom-Feeders

The elevator returned us to the alley where we hid from Elena. It was cold, we were wet, and we needed a hiding place. *Quick.*

"I'm starving! Let's get some bagels."

Zoe shivered. "Good idea. It's always warm in Pick a Bagel. Let's go."

We jetted around the corner and into the busy shop, trying our best to ignore the stares of the dry New Yorkers in the bagel line.

"Man, you guys are lucky you were in here!" Doug, never shy in the face of food, says to the crowd. "You missed the cloud burst!"

A woman, sitting in a corner booth drinking a steaming coffee, brought a blanket to Zoe and placed it around her shoulders. "Here you go, sweetie. You can keep this. You always need to be prepared with a rain poncho or umbrella around here." Then she handed me a twenty. "Have a nice evening." Her eyes glued to my chest. "My, that's a nice medallion."

I reached for Triple T and dropped it under my soggy clothes. "Thanks."

We sat in that warm bagel shop for at least an hour, too scared to go out in the freezing winter afternoon.

"How long do you think it would take us to ice over out there?" Doug asked.

"Two minutes." Michael stood up. "Tell you what I'm going to do." He put his hand to his chin. "I'm going to go find us all some dry clothes."

"What?" Zoe pulled the blanket a little tighter around her shoulders.

"Wait here!" Michael disappeared out the door. We stayed tight, sitting close together for warmth. About thirty minutes later, Michael returned with a bag of clothes.

"Where did you get these?" Zoe reached in and pulled out some jeans, a big fluffy sweater, a beanie, and a pair of snow boots.

Michael smiled. "My church! We have a closet full of clothes for people in need. I think the fact that we're soaked puts us in that category. Pastor Dave was happy to let me borrow some. I hope I guessed your sizes right."

Zoe hugged the clothes. "This is the most thoughtful thing anyone has ever done for me." She smiled and headed into the bathroom.

One by one, we changed our clothes in the cramped

bagel shop, which gave us time to fill our stomachs with lots of bread, cream cheese, and hot chocolate.

"We better get back," Zoe said, "or we'll be late for dinner."

"Late for dinner? I'm starving!" Doug rubbed his belly.

"Doug, you just ate." I gathered up our bagel wrappings and headed for the trash.

"I just ate? Nah, I'm just gettin' started! I just paddled across the Amazon River, ya know."

When we reached 88th Street, we said goodbye to Michael Tolley and climbed up the steps to our brownstone, where we found a pink bakery box sitting on the welcome mat. It had Elena's sticky note attached to it.

"How did she find out where I live?" I lifted the lid of the box and inhaled deeply.

Cinnamon rolls. Yum.

They were a little cold from sitting out, but I was sure I could polish them off.

There was a second note attached to the inside lid.

Dear Arcade,
I am SO sorry I ruined your glasses.
PLEASE, let me buy you a new pair. Also,
please accept these cinnamon rolls as
a peace offering. Your twin uncles were
nice enough to show me where you live.

I was lucky to meet them out front as I was roaming the neighborhood, hoping to find you.
See you tomorrow at school.

Warmly, Elena S.C.

Twin uncles?

"Zoe, unlock the door, quick! We gotta get out of sight."

Zoe fumbled through her purse for her key. "What's the matter?"

"I'll tell you when we get inside."

Zoe opened the door, and I practically pushed her and Doug through. I locked the door behind us and we rushed upstairs to my room.

"Twin uncles?" Zoe scratched her head as she read Elena's note. "We don't have twin uncles."

"I know! But we've got a couple sets of twins in our lives. And I don't feel good about either one of them."

Doug lifted the bakery box lid and shoved a finger into the cream cheese frosting. "I bet it was the Tolleys. That makes the most sense. They live on our street."

"But *uncles*? They're a little young to be uncles, don't you think?"

Doug brushed me off. "Oh, no, I have a nephew who's thirty years old."

"Huh?" Zoe and I both looked at him.

"Long story I'd rather not get into."

"Well," Zoe sat down on my bed, "I guess it's possible. But why would the Tolleys tell Elena that they were your uncles, Arcade?"

"They like to mess with people." Doug licked his fingers. "Seems normal to me."

"But you have to see *this*." I rustled through papers on my desk and produced the card. "Here." I handed it to Zoe, but Doug intercepted it.

"Awww, man, you got a card from Miss Gertrude? I didn't get a card from her on my birthday. You think she forgot about me?"

Zoe pulled the card from Doug. "Miss Gertrude?" She pored over the words of the card, and followed the squiggly arrow to the shocking P.S.

"They're back!?! The Badgers are back? Why didn't you tell me, Arcade?"

"I sort of forgot, with the birthday surprise, the run around New York City, and then today. Today was the longest Monday of my li—"

Zoe got all up in my grill. "Do you think they're back HERE? In New York City?"

"I was trying to tell you just now that I haven't had time to think about it."

"Maybe they were the ones on our street earlier when Elena was looking for you. This is NOT good, Arcade!"

"I agree."

Doug took a big bite of cinnamon roll. "Hey, you guys just agreed on something!" Then he walked over to our bedroom window that looks out on 88th Street.

Zoe whipped out her phone and started poking her screen.

"What are you doing?"

"I'm calling Miss Gertrude! We have to know where the Badger brothers are!"

Doug reached up, pulled the blinds down, and turned around, eyes wide. "No need. One of them is down there." He pointed a finger to the floor.

"Down where?" I asked, my voice shaking.

"Down on the street. Walking up the stairs to our house. It's getting dark, but I can tell it's a Badger."

"Just one?"

"That's all I could see."

Someone rang the doorbell. Loopy barked and ran downstairs.

We all froze.

Doug peeked out the cracks of the blinds. "It's him but . . . *this* is interesting. One of the Tolleys is walking up the stairs too."

"Just one?"

"You already asked me that."

"I was talking about the Badger brother."

Doug nodded. "Oh. Yeah."

"This is crazy," Zoe whispered.

"And we don't even know which Badger brother this is."

"Doesn't matter," Zoe said. "They're all bottom-feeders."

Doug kept peeking. "Now they're laughing." He squinted. "I wonder what they're talking about?"

I squeezed my eyes shut. "I don't even want to think about it. I hope he's not telling him about the token. That's all I need, four brothers after me."

"Hey," Doug said. "We already got one Tolley who knows. So that would make five."

Zoe put a hand on her hip. "Michael will *never* tell. And he would never try to take the token."

"Well, don't make him mad, Zoe, or he might." I paced around, moved toward the window, and then stepped back.

"Mad? How could I make him mad?"

"Just being yourself. You make me mad all the time."

"*You're* mad, Arcade."

Doug held a hand up in the air. "Hey, guys, stop for a minute. The streetlights just came on . . ." he leaned closer toward the window ". . . looks like they're finishing their conversation . . . there's a fist bump . . . and . . ."

"And what?"

Doug turned around. "They're gone. Each one went a separate direction."

"Everyone who does evil hates the light . . ." Zoe stood up and walked over to look out the blinds. ". . . for fear that their deeds will be exposed." She turned to me. "Just like your river monster, Arcade, the light scared them away."

I sat down next to her and dropped my head in my hands. "But why would evil ring the doorbell?"

When we were sure there were no twins in sight, we snuck down the stairs and cracked the front door open. An envelope fell to the ground. It had some scrawled handwriting on the front that said ARCADE.

I kicked it inside the house and closed the door quickly. We all just stared at it for a moment.

"Belated birthday card?" Doug chuckled.

"Not likely." Zoe picked it up.

"Um, it's addressed to me."

She handed it over. I walked over to the living room couch and Zoe and Doug followed, wedging themselves on either side of me.

"Space, people. I need space." I wiggled my shoulders until they moved over. I ripped the envelope open, pulled out a small index card, and read it out loud.

"Arcade—LB wants it. You should keep it. Caught in between. Need help.—KB"

A phone number was scratched at the bottom.

"KB? You think that was Kenwood Badger ringing our doorbell?" Zoe took the card from me to examine it more closely.

"Bawk! Listen to Zoe! Listen to Zoe!"

I shook my head. "You've taught your bird some really annoying phrases, Zoe."

"You mean *truthful* phrases, don't you?"

"Why would Kenwood Badger be asking *me* for help? What am I supposed to do?"

Doug took the card from Zoe to look at it. "It sounds like he disagrees with his brother about the token."

"But when my sister and I disagree, I just argue until I set her straight."

"Haha. I'm the one who sets *you* straight, and you know it." Zoe and I got into a little shoulder-nudging, but then I stopped and took the note back from Doug.

I read it again. "How do we know this isn't a setup?"

"We don't." Zoe plucked the card from my hand and paced the living room. "So that's why we should ignore it. Just like before. Remember, Arcade? When Lenwood Badger was bothering us? We blocked all his calls."

Doug pointed to the paper. "But this is *Kenwood*. And he wants you to call *him*."

Zoe rolled her eyes and ripped up the card. "And now he's blocked."

Zoe's the best! Zoe's the best!

CHAPTER 15
Dodging

For the rest of the week, all my energy was spent dodging people.

The Tolleys asked me if I would go on another trip to the library with them.

"Sorry, guys. Card's still blocked." And I scooted away.

And every time I came out of my brownstone, I looked both ways for Badgers. Since it was January and most people were wearing big coats and hoods, I had to be extra watchful.

But the hardest person to dodge was Elena Salvador Castro. The girl would not stop with the gifts.

On Tuesday, she left chocolate chip cookies on my desk in Mr. Dooley's class.

"SECRET ADMIRER, MR. LIVINGSTON? CARE TO SHARE?" Mr. Dooley came over to my desk and I gave him a cookie. He munched it down and smiled. "SHE'S A KEEPER."

On Wednesday, she slipped a gift card for movie tickets into my locker, with a note:

> *Want new glasses to watch the movie?*
> *Call me!*

But the most shocking gift was the one waiting on my front doorstep when I got home from school on Thursday.

"Dude, you keep gettin' stuff!" Doug ran to the kitchen for an after-school snack. "Wish I had some glasses for her to bust."

I plopped my backpack on the floor and placed the heavy box on the dining room table before joining Doug in the kitchen.

"Aren't you going to open it?"

"Not till after I have some food."

"But it might BE food. Remember the cookies." Doug went over to the package and sniffed it.

I threw my head back. "Okaaaaay, but you have to help me figure out how to get rid of that girl."

"Maybe there'll be a clue in here." Doug lifted the box and shook it. "It's heavy. Maybe it's books!"

I ripped off the wrapping paper, revealing a cardboard box secured with packing tape. I loosened the tape until I could open the flaps. Inside, I found another, *bigger* neon pink sticky note:

> *YOU'LL NEED NEW GLASSES TO READ*
> *THESE. CALL ME!*
>
>   *ESC*

Under the note was a pair of crazy socks with pairs of glasses on them. Under the socks were three books. *Ancient Greek Architecture*, *Greek Craftsmen*, and . . . *Arcadia Adventures*.

Goosebumps popped up all over my body. I dug in my backpack for my phone.

"Where's Elena's sticky note?"

"Where's Elena's sticky note?"

"That's what I said, Doug! Where is it?"

"The one with her phone number on it? I thought you wanted to get rid of her."

"Not anymore. Where is it?"

"Well, um . . . I think it was attached to the cinnamon roll box she left for you."

"And where is that?"

Doug licked his lips.

"Where is it, Doug?"

"In the trash. I threw it away after I polished off the cinnamon rolls."

"You know I didn't get *one* bite of those?"

"I didn't think you wanted them!"

I waved a hand in the air. "Never mind, come help me dig through the trash."

About three-quarters of the way into the trash bin, we found the pink box with a few stale crumbs inside and the sticky note!

"I gotta call her." I ran inside the house . . . right into Mom!

"Hey, honey." She sniffed me and peeled off a gum wrapper that was stuck to my sleeve. "Have you been digging in the trash?"

"Mom! You're *never* home this early." I carefully pushed the sticky note into my hoodie pocket.

Mom pulled out a dining room chair, sat down, and ran a hand through her hair. "I know. It's a miracle. I finally had an afternoon with no meetings, so I decided to come home and hang out with my favorite kids. Does someone want to make me some tea?"

"I got you, Mrs. L." Doug went into the kitchen and filled up the tea kettle. "Orange Pekoe?"

Mom smiled. "That would be nice. And I think I have some shortbread cookies in the pantry. Arcade, are you all right?" She examined me carefully. "Are your glasses *broken*?"

I started to tell her about the awesome block that I made with my face when she spotted the box. She pulled it closer and peered in.

"Ooooh. Has someone been shopping online for books? And socks?" She raised an eyebrow. "Hope you haven't been using my account for this."

"No, ma'am. It was a gift."

"Ah. birthday gifts are the best." She pulled the books out one by one. "Greece? That's an interesting country." She focused closely on the book about Arcadia. "I have . . . I mean, I could have taken you to the library."

"Nah, he's got a blocked card." Doug poured steaming water into my mom's favorite teacup.

Mom leaned back in her chair and crossed her arms. "Blocked? That doesn't sound like you, Arcade."

"It wasn't me, Mom. It was Zoe."

"No need to blame your sister. Either way, sometimes

it's nice to *buy* books. Hey," she snapped her fingers, "you can put them in between your new bookends! They're still in my tote from the other night. I'll unwrap them later and put them up on your bookshelf."

"Thanks, Mom."

I grabbed the box and took it to the upstairs landing.

Out of sight, out of mind . . . I hope.

At that moment, the front door swung open and in walked Zoe. She saw Mom and ran over to give her a big hug. "I'm so glad you're home."

"Me too. It's about time I came home at a reasonable hour. Want to join me for tea?" Mom pulled away from Zoe to get a look at her face. "Honey, what's wrong?"

"Michael and I got in a fight."

I dropped the box.

"Uh, well, I'm outta here." I pointed a thumb toward the stairs. "C'mon, Doug, we have some homework to do."

Zoe wiped a tear with the heel of her hand. "Since when do you do homework right after school?"

Mom reached over and rubbed Zoe's arm. "They're letting us have some girl time." She turned to me. "I'll bring those bookends up later."

"Thanks."

I ran up the stairs.

I threw the box of books on my bed and sat down on my desk chair to catch my breath. Loopy came out from under my bed and jumped up on my lap. "It's all closing in, Loop. I gotta figure out the truth about this token soon."

I reached into my pocket and took out my phone and Elena's note. I squinted through my dusty lenses, sweating a little as I punched in the numbers.

The phone rang three times, four times.

"Hello, unknown number. This better be Arcade and not a robo-call." Elena laughed on the other end. "Hello?"

Oh, right. I'm supposed to talk.

"Hi. This is Arcade."

"Finally! I figured the books would throw you over the edge. You ready to take the new glasses, or should I keep stalking you?"

"How did you get my school schedule? How do you know chocolate chip cookies are my favorite? And why did you give me books about Greece?"

"Hmmm, let's see, I watched you walk into Dooley's on Tuesday morning, the chocolate chip cookies were a guess, and I'll tell you about the books when you meet me at 575 Columbus Avenue tomorrow at four o'clock."

"What's at 575 Columbus Avenue?"

"My dad's office. He's an *optometrist*. And it's right near the corner of 88th Street where you live. So, no excuses."

"That's blackmail."

"Blackmail? *Blackmail?* I'm trying to do something *nice* for you, Livingston. Plus, you look ridiculous with that tape on your glasses. And have you thought that maybe God let that volleyball hit you in the face for a reason?

Stop fighting the process and just meet me at four o'clock tomorrow."

Click.

"Oh, no, you are not allowed to just hang up on me." I poked the redial button and tried to figure out what I would say in response. Like . . .

Oh, yeah? Well, maybe I like the way my broken glasses look!

But the phone just rang and rang. "You better pick up, Elena Salvador Castro."

It rang and rang some more. Then finally:

"Hello, you've reached Elena. I'm sorry I missed your call. Please leave a message, and may God shine his light all over your day."

BEEEEEP!

"Elena!" I yelled into the phone, scaring Loopy back under the bed.

"Who are you yelling at?" Doug came in the door.

"That annoying girl! She just tricked me into going to her dad's optometry office to get new glasses tomorrow."

Doug walked over to me and pulled off my glasses. "Tricked you, huh? How long have you had these? They're all scratched, did you know that?"

"They are?"

Doug tried to look at me through them. "Yeah. Like, really scratched!" Then he bent them at the middle. The tape broke and he was holding two pieces. "Yeah, she's a really annoying girl."

"Doug! I need those."

"No worries, man. I got more tape." Doug walked over

to the desk we share and pulled some duct tape out of the drawer. He pulled off a skinny piece and wrapped it around the nosepiece. "There. The silver is less noticeable than that white athletic tape."

I popped the glasses back on my face. "Thanks." Then I squinted at Doug. "These *are* scratched, aren't they?"

"They've been taking a beating. Hey—what kind of coincidence is it that her dad's a glasses guy?" Doug jumped up on his bunk, laid down, and folded his hands behind his head. "You know what? You should see if she can get you an extra pair. With that token, you never know what's gonna happen."

"Okay, *now* you're pushing it." I sat down on my bed and took the books out of the box, paying close attention to *Arcadia Adventures*. I pulled the Triple T Token out from under my shirt, turned it to the back and compared the book title to the bottom inscription on the token: *Arcade Adventures*.

Arcadia, Greece. Arcade Adventures. My name is Arcade. It can't be coincidence!

I opened the book to try to read it, but it was all a blur.

"Doug! I can't read!"

Doug sat up and bumped his head on the ceiling. "Ouch! What do you mean, you can't read?"

"My eyes . . . these glasses . . . the dim light . . ." I moved over to the window and pulled the blinds up. "I wish the days were longer in January. Everything gets dark so early around here."

"You could flip the light switch on."

"True." Zoe's hand reached in through the cracked bedroom door. She flipped the light switch. "What's going on in here?" She walked in the room. Her eyes were red.

"Do you think Michael will tell his brothers about the token now that he's mad at you?"

Doug isn't known for having the best timing, but even I cringed at the question.

Zoe sat down and started to cry again. "No. He won't say a thing. He's the nicest, most honest boy . . ."

Okay, okay. Enough with the sap.

". . . but we keep having arguments. He says that I'm strong-willed, that I always have to be right about everything. He said that I'm the *stubbornest* person he's ever met. And 'stubbornest' isn't even grammatically correct!"

Stubborn-est?

"Oh, I think it is." My token began to flash. I covered it with my hand. "But what guy wouldn't want a girlfriend like that?" I went over and ruffled her bangs.

She pushed my hand away. "Don't try to be nice right now, Arcade. I know you agree with Michael."

I sighed. "You know what we all need? A long break. Some time to figure things out. I feel like things are closing in all around us. I was just telling Loopy—"

"Arcade! Look at your hand!" Doug jumped off his bunk and moved in closer. "It's glowing!"

Sure enough, the light from the token was shining through my hand. As soon as I took my hand away, dazzling lights filled the room.

"Everybody, grab your backpacks. Bring some notepads and pens." I reached for the cardboard box filled with the Greece books. As I did, lights shot out toward my closet, turning it into a golden elevator. The coin slot, with the sign GET TRUTH, slid down from the ceiling this time. The coin slot gleamed, and a golden beam of light shot out toward the token. "Maybe bring a waterproof coat too."

Zoe gathered some tissues to wipe her eyes, then ran into her room and came back with her coat. I dug the duct tape out of my desk drawer . . . just in case.

"Wait! I got something for you, Arcade!" Doug pulled the bottom desk drawer open and brought out a gift bag. "Here. Happy birthday."

"Doug, I told you I didn't need a gift."

"Yeah, but we're headed out somewhere and it could come in handy."

I reached into the middle of the tissue paper and pulled out a . . . pocket knife?

"Doug! How did you kno—"

Zoe poked me in the ribs. "Hey, the coin slot is fading. Better throw Triple T in there." She pointed to my new knife. "And don't get ANY ideas about some new haircut, unless it's for you."

I gripped the knife tight, sliding it in my hoodie pocket.

Then I pulled the token from the chain. "Take us on a long break." I dropped the token in the slot. "And take us somewhere light enough for me to read, so I can get some truth about Greece." I handed the books to Zoe, pushed my palms together, then pulled them apart, and the antique elevator doors rolled open.

"I love this family." Doug ran in.

I looked at Zoe. "Me too."

She sniffed. "No matter what happens, I've got your back."

I smiled. "And I've got yours."

We were in the same elevator as before, with the domed ceiling and the statues and plaques up high. "This is three times now. Ruah must be trying to tell me something."

"It sure is a beautiful sight," Zoe said. "I feel joy when I look at it. Not sure why. Maybe because it's so bright."

Doug sat down on the floor. "It would be nice if this adventure didn't include a large drop-off or a scary ledge."

I sat down next to Doug. "I asked for light, and I asked for a long break. We'll see what we get."

The ride was a little longer than usual, so I took out the books for Doug and Zoe to see. And we filled Doug in on some important information.

"So, you went to Greece and you met a kid who made the Triple T mold?" Doug flipped through the pages of *Greek Craftsmen*.

"No, I didn't actually meet him. I talked to Ruah—"

"Who's Ruah?"

"The Triple T woman," Zoe answered. "That's her name. Ruah."

"That's a weird name. Does it mean something?"

Zoe and I dropped our books and looked at Doug.

"What did you say?"

"I said, does it mean something?"

Zoe smacked her head with the palm of her hand. "Of course! It has to! That's genius, Doug! Let's look it up!" We all took our phones out of our backpacks and poked at our screens. And, as usual, they didn't work.

"Guess we'll look it up after our long break." Doug threw his phone back into his backpack. "Kinda freeing, not having to check our phones, isn't it?"

Zoe sighed and stretched her arms. "Yeah. Must be what it was like in the good old days."

A soothing song played over the loudspeaker.

"Elevator music." Doug laid down on the floor. "It's making me kinda tired."

In fact, it made *all* of us tired. We propped our coats up like pillows and closed our eyes. And we slept for a while. I know, because when the elevator dinged, I had some drool coming out of the corner of my mouth.

I wipe the drool and check on both sides of me. Zoe and Doug are asleep.

"Hey! You guys!" I shake them both. "We're here!"

Zoe sits up. "Where? Where are we?"

Doug jumps. "What? We're here? Cool!"

We stand and gather our stuff. The elevator opens to a

sun-filled view of a quaint city. Businesses line both sides of the road.

Zoe rubs her arms. "It's chilly." She puts on her coat. "Why is it so quiet?" She points up at a huge clock at the end of the street. "It's two o'clock and there's no one around."

Doug laughs. "Well, then, we sure aren't in New York City!"

"I'm not sure where to go," I admit with a shrug.

Doug points to a café about halfway down the empty street. "Anyone bring money? I'm hungry."

Zoe pulls her backpack off her shoulders. "I have some."

The café is called Chill 23. We open the door and are greeted by a young thirty-something woman who is sweeping the floor. Chairs are turned upside-down on the round café tables.

The woman keeps sweeping. "Sorry, we're closing." She looks up and her eyes widen. "*Children?* Why are you out? It's way past curfew."

"I'm sorry," I say. "Why do you close at two o'clock in the afternoon?"

The woman rests her broom against the counter and walks toward us. "Two in the *afternoon?* No. It's two o'clock *in the morning.* Where do you think you are?"

I look out the window to make sure I haven't gone crazy. "But the sun is out."

The woman chuckles. "Tell me about it. I'd like it to go down, but that's not going to happen for a while."

"A while?" Zoe looks at me. "How *far* north are we?"

I turn to the woman, hoping she won't call the

authorities if I can come up with a good story. "I'm sorry. We just got off a long . . . uh . . . plane ride. We're trying to get our bearings. Can you help us figure out where we are, and where we can find a place to rest?"

The woman looks at us through narrowed eyes. Then her suspicious gaze softens, and she pulls some chairs down from the tables so we can sit. "You kids drink coffee?"

We shake our heads.

"How about milkshakes?"

"Yep!" Doug says.

"Gotcha. Three solstice specials, coming right up."

"Solstice?" Doug rubs his belly. "Sounds yummy. What's in that?"

The woman leans with her elbows on the counter. "A whole lot of sugar, so you can stay up for twenty-four hours."

"Sounds perfect. But why would we want to stay up for twenty-four hours?"

The woman shakes her head and begins to mix the milkshakes. "Because this is Reykjavík, Iceland, and you've arrived on June twenty-first. The *longest* day of the year *anywhere*! That sun is not going to go down tonight."

Long-EST!

"Iceland? Really? That's dope!"

Zoe kicks me behind the counter. "My brother is jet-lagged. He's been excited about our trip to Iceland. So much, that he can hardly believe we're finally here. And the light outside really threw all of us off. We actually just woke up after sleeping all night . . . or day . . . well, I'm not really sure. See what I mean?"

The woman finishes blending the shakes and brings the silver container on a platter, with three glasses, to the café table. There's something in her smirk that tells me she isn't going to rat us out.

"My name is Katrin." She pours milkshakes in all our glasses. "Welcome to Iceland, Land of Fire *and* Ice."

"Thank you." I sit down and pick up one of the glasses. "We're honored to be here." I take a swallow of the shake. "I read once that Greenland has more ice than Iceland, and Iceland is greener than Greenland. I love facts like that."

Katrin laughs. "Yes, that is a strange fact."

"I'm sorry we barged in on you as you were closing up."

"It's quite fine." Katrin takes a seat. "I think it was meant to be. I had a little spill in the kitchen that kept me here later than usual. What are your names?"

"I'm Arcade, this is my sister, Zoe, and this is our soon-to-be brother, Doug."

Katrin nods and smiles. "Sounds like a heartwarming story in there somewhere. If I may ask, what's in the box?"

I go get the box that I left on the counter.

"Oh, that's just some books," Doug says. "Arcade's a booklover."

Katrin's eyes light up. "I love to read too! Are they books about Iceland?"

"Uh, no." I open the flaps and pull one out.

"Then what?"

"They're books about Greece. It's hard to explain." I reach up and run my fingers over the empty chain under my sweatshirt.

Katrin puts a hand out. "Bookworms should never have to explain why they are reading a certain book. Read what you're curious about and what brings you joy. That's my motto. Right now, I'm reading a Christmas book, and look at it outside! Summer for days and days and days. In six months, it will be nothing but winter. That's when I fell in love with books as a kid. During those long, cold winter days."

I put my Greece book back in the box. "I like you, Katrin."

She laughs. "Thank you! Your visit has made my day. And since it's the longest day ever, that's a good thing."

We finish up our shakes while Katrin does a little more cleaning of the café.

"What do we owe you?" Zoe pulls her wallet out of her backpack. "I'm sorry, all I have are American dollars."

"On the house," Katrin says. We thank her, and we're just about to turn to leave when she asks, "Do you children have a place to stay? I'm assuming that your parents are on a . . . delayed flight, perhaps?" Before we get a chance to answer, Katrin picks up a phone behind the counter. "Hello, this is Katrin, over at Chill 23. Is Ruah there?"

Ruah?!?

"Hello, Ruah. Do you have any vacancies? I have three children here . . . they just got in . . . yes. Their parents are delayed. I know . . . you do? Can I drop them off in a few minutes? That would be wonderful! Thank you so much."

Katrin hangs up. "There's a room waiting for you at the Northern Lights Hotel. I would like to drive you so you don't get picked up by the curfew police. My friend Ruah has set it all up. All you have to do is go to the front desk and ask for the key."

"Thank you, Katrin," Zoe says. "You're an angel."

I just have to ask. "Ruah? That's such an unusual name. Do you know if it means something?"

Katrin smiles. "A beautiful name, indeed. It means 'breath' or 'spirit.' In some contexts, it refers to the Holy Spirit."

The woman who meets us at the desk is not Ruah. It's someone named Margret.

"Welcome, weary travelers!" She looks behind us. "No luggage?"

Doug nods. "We travel light. Except for Arcade's books." He points to my cardboard box.

"I have your key cards right here. You'll be in room 230, which has a beautiful view of the sun shining on our city. It's our Solstice Suite Special."

Doug chuckles. "Wow. This town has a lot of specials."

Margret scribbles our room number on the key envelope. "Yes, but I do have some bad news. The room was available because we had the blackout blinds sent out for cleaning. I'm sorry, but you won't be able to darken the room to sleep."

"That's okay," Zoe says. "We got a lot of sleep on the elev—"

"PLANE," I interrupt, drowning out Zoe's voice.

The woman winks at Zoe. "That's what I hoped. The

good news is, this is a twenty-four hour rental, so your checkout time won't be until three o'clock tomorrow."

"How are we going to know it's tomorrow if it doesn't get dark?"

Great question, Doug!

Margret laughs. "We can send you a wake-up call an hour before checkout if you like."

"That's perfect. That will give us a nice long break to read," I say. "Thank you so much, ma'am. What do we owe you?" I gesture to Zoe, the one with the money. She gives me a funny look and pulls out her wallet.

Margret puts her palms up. "Paid for by my good friend Ruah. She had to go, but she told me to tell you, 'Happy travels, and I will see you soon.'" She pulls a paper from behind the desk and hands it to Doug. "Here's our restaurant menu. Your package includes twenty-four-hour, all-you-can-eat room service. So don't leave here hungry, okay?"

Doug's eyes light up almost as bright as the Triple T Token. "OKAY!"

"Arcade, this is the best long break ever!" Doug pulls open the sheer curtains in our suite and we all stare out at the sun.

"Can you believe it's . . . what time is it?" I look at the alarm clock next to the hotel bed. "Three-fifteen? In the morning? This could really mess with a person."

Zoe falls back in a comfortable recliner chair. "This is

nice. Getting away from all the stress. Ever since that token came into our lives, it's been one crazy trip after another."

"Zoe, *this* is a crazy trip. And as soon as we get back, we'll be right back into it again. We have to find out about the maker of the Triple T mold." I walk over to the coffee table and pull the three books out of the box, giving *Ancient Greek Architecture* to Doug and *Greek Craftsmen* to Zoe while keeping *Arcadia Adventures* for myself.

I sigh. "Now *this* is the life. A nice bright hotel room and a bunch of good books. Enjoy!"

I plop on my back on the bed and pull all the pillows in behind me. I crack open the book, looking for a clue, any clue, about ancient Greece, metalworking, and a boy who always works.

But all I see is a blur.

"Hey! What's going on here?" I pull my glasses off my face and wipe the lenses with my sweatshirt. I try them on again. Nothing! I wipe them with the edge of the pillowcase. Nothing but blur!

"This is cool, Arcade. It says here that the ancient Greeks invented the theater. So they were the first Broadway! This New York City boy feels a connection already." Doug jumps on my bed and shakes me. "Arcade? Did you hear what I said?"

I look up. "Yes, I did. Broadway. Theater. Yeah . . . huh."

"What's wrong?"

"Arcade?" Zoe is sitting next to me now. "Are you sick?"

I take my glasses off and pull the book as close to my face

as I can. But it doesn't matter. I can't read the words on any of the pages.

"I'm having a problem with my glasses. Or something. This is really frustrating."

Zoe retrieves her book from the recliner. "Here, try this one. The font is a little larger. I'll turn the light on brighter." She clicks the lamp a couple of notches until it blasts me like a surveillance light at a police station. "With that in here and the sun out there, you have to be able to see it."

I focus, squint, and stare. "Nothing."

"I don't get it, Arcade. You could see the time on the clock. Am *I* blurry?" Zoe waves her hands around. "How about Doug?"

I look at both of them. "No, you guys are clear."

"Man, it's a good thing you're seeing Elena's dad tomorrow."

I try to shush Doug, but it's too late. Zoe pounces.

"Really? *Elena's* dad? Why are you going to see *him*?"

"Calm down, Zoe. Her dad's an optometrist. He's going to get me some new glasses."

"Oh, I see."

"No, Zoe. *I* need to see. That's why I'm going. Plus, Elena promised to tell me how she knew to give me these books on Greece. She can't, you know, *know*, can she?"

"Well, she *has* been stalking you," Doug says, "and it seems just about everyone knows about it now." He counts on his fingers as he names some names. "The Badgers, Michael Tolley, and now probably Kevin or Casey. Whichever one Kenwood Badger was talking to on our front porch."

I lay back on the pillows and stare up at the ceiling. "It's just like I said, things are closing in! I've gotta find out the truth about Triple T."

"What kind of truth?" Doug asks.

"Why do *I* have it? And what's the *purpose*? I have to find that boy."

Zoe removes the useless Greece book from my lap. "Well, right now we can't do that. So we might as well enjoy the nice accommodations."

I sit up and think for a minute, then it hits me. "Zoe, you might be right for once. Since we can't read, let's go explore Iceland!"

Zoe points to the clock. "We can't, remember? Curfew. It's still night."

Well, the sun has a funny way of showing it.

Doug orders up some great Icelandic food—hot dogs—from the twenty-four-hour room service, and we munch away while we watch the sun pretty much not move.

"Light is interesting, isn't it?" Zoe washes her hot dog down with a swig of water. "I feel so much better than I did at home. I wonder if they have much crime here in Reykjavík in the summer? I mean, you can see everything, and evil hates the light."

"I wouldn't want to be here in the winter then," Doug says.

I scratch my head. "Yeah, but then it's *cold*. And you

heard what Katrin said. Everyone *reads* in the winter. Readers don't become criminals. I'd love to be here in the winter, but with new glasses!"

We sit in silence for a few moments, taking in the light from the long-EST day in the world.

"Hey, guys," Doug sits up on the bed and turns around to face us. "I have to tell you something."

His voice sounds crackly, and kind of serious. Which is not normal for Doug.

Zoe leans forward. "What's up, Doug?"

He clears his throat and looks down at his hands that are folded over his crossed legs on the bed. "I got a call from my gram's care facility. I tried to tell you about it the other day, Arcade, but we got interrupted by Elena."

My stomach turns. "The disturbing call?"

How could I forget about that?

"Yeah, that one."

Zoe reaches out and puts a hand on Doug's shoulder. "Is your gram okay?"

I'm afraid to hear the answer.

"She's . . . her body is working okay. And she likes the place. It's just . . ."

"What Doug? You can tell us. We're here to help with anything." I run my fingers over my empty gold chain.

Doug rubs the back of his neck. "Thanks, Arcade, but there's really nothing you can do. There's not really much I can do either, since . . ."

"Since what?" I stare out into the bright night in Reykjavík.

No darkness can possibly find us here. Can it?

"Gram's been forgetting things."

I sigh. "Ah. Older people forget sometimes. My grandma says it's because they have so many wonderful memories, and their brains need room for those, so they forget unimportant things. Like where their keys are. Stuff like that."

Zoe shakes her head at me and puts a finger to her lips. "Go on, Doug. What is she forgetting?"

Doug drops his chin and holds his head in his hands. "Big things. Like what city she lives in. What her name is. And . . . that she has a grandson. They're doing tests to find out what's wrong, but the people at the facility asked me not to visit until they can get her stabilized. I guess she's really upset all the time."

More silence.

Doug wipes a couple of tears that escape down his cheek. "Is this how it's all going to end? With Gram not knowing who I am, and then I'm just supposed to forget about her? I can't do that, you guys. She's too special."

"Of course she is," Zoe says. "And no, that's *not* how it's going to end."

"How do you know?"

Zoe has a tear dropping down her cheek now too. She puts her hand on her heart. "Because I know *you*. And because . . . I just know. You'll have to trust me."

Doug sits up a little straighter on the bed. "Okay. Since you're my almost-big-sister, I will. After all, you're always right, right?" One side of his mouth turns up in a grin, then goes back to a frown. "There is one more disturbing thing."

"We'll get through it," Zoe says.

Doug takes a deep breath and lets it out. "My aunt found out about Gram. She's asking for custody of me since Gram can't make good decisions about the adoption right now."

"What?" I jump to my feet. "But *we're* going to adopt you! Your gram said it was okay! It is better for you to stay in New York and—"

"Gram hasn't signed the final paperwork for the adoption yet, and if she doesn't know who I am . . ."

"No! This isn't happening!" I start to pace the room.

My first sleepless solstice is supposed to be an adventure, not a nightmare.

I stop at the window and stare out into the bright sunlight.

What can I do? If only time would stand still . . .

I glance over at the clock. It's five o'clock.

Some people get up this early to go to work. Curfew has to be over by now.

I feel a gust of wind brush by my cheek, which is weird since we're inside.

Did I just feel . . . a breath?

I run for the door. "You two stay here, I'll be right back."

"Arcade! You better not leave the hote—"

The heavy hotel door slams behind me, cutting off Zoe's words. I jog down the long hallway to the elevator. I push the button—*How cool it is to use a normal elevator?*—and wait for the doors to open. They do, and there stands Ruah! She's wearing the white sweat suit and the Triple T ballcap, but this time she looks like she's around my mom's age.

"Thanks for the nice solstice room," I stammer.

"You're welcome. Why aren't you in it with your sister and Doug?"

"I was on my way to the front desk. To look for you."

"To thank me for the room?"

"Well, yes. But, no. I wanted to ask you why *I* have the Triple T Token. And who the boy is who made the mold. And are you some kind of spirit?"

Ruah smiles. "Arcade, you have traveled and you have been tested. You *will* know why you have the token when you have discovered the truth about yourself."

"The truth about myself? Wait! I had a dream about that!"

"Good! And what did you find out?"

"I didn't. I woke up! And in my dream, I couldn't read or see anything. It was frustrating, Ruah! I wanted to see!"

She grins and nods. "You have gone wide and you have gone long. You must go high first, then deep. Soon you will see *everything*."

A familiar ding sounds from inside the elevator.

"No! Don't leave yet!"

I try to step in, but an invisible barrier stops me. I press my palms against it. "Ruah! I have more questions!"

She laughs. "Of course you do. Your name is Arcade Livingston, is it not? You have the wrong elevator, my friend." She points to the elevator across the hall. Then the doors close, and she's gone.

"Arcade!" Zoe runs down the hallway. "You can't just leave like that!"

Doug follows, right at her heels. "Dude, no Icelandic adventures without us!"

I pace back and forth in the hallway. "Sorry, guys. I just had a feeling Ruah was in the building, and I had to catch her."

Zoe looks around. "Well, did you?"

"Only for a minute! She *never* answers my questions! And she told me that I had the wrong elevato—"

Just as I say that, I feel a heavy clunk on my chest.

Oh, no. I want this day to be longer!

"It's back, Arcade." Doug taps the front of my black T-shirt. A bright light is shining through it.

Triple T has returned.

And the dark, quiet elevator Ruah pointed to is now gleaming light out of the cracks in the antique golden doors.

"Time to go back already?" Zoe steps up next to me.

The button on the wall next to the elevator turns into a coin slot, and light pulsates from it toward the token. Golden words flicker on the marquis above the doors. GET TRUTH.

"I need to go high, and I need to go deep. But before I do that, I need some new glasses." I step forward, closer to the slot. "Please, take us home." I reach inside my shirt and pull out the token. I give it a tug. It comes right off. Just like always.

"Not sure I'm ready to leave this bright place," Zoe says.

I put a hand on her shoulder as I drop the coin in the slot. "Guess we'll just have to take some of this light back with us."

The token makes a clunk as it falls through the slot.

Is it going back to the mold? And if so, why?

The strange breeze hits my cheeks again as I make the open-door motion with my hands. The antique doors slide open. The elevator is bright inside.

I raise my palms to the ceiling. "Ready to get back to reality?"

Doug straightens up. "Ready to get back to reality? Which one is reality? Here? Or there?"

I push him into the elevator. "Dude, I'm the one who's supposed to ask the questions."

You ou sure you don't want us to go with you?" Zoe and Doug walked on either side of me as we climbed the stairs to our brownstone after school on Friday.

"You know I love both of you, but this girl is tough. I need all my concentration to deal with her nonsense. You," I point to Doug, "would just distract me. And you," I point to Zoe, "are the stubborn-est. Though you might have a contender for that title."

"But what if the token lights up?" Zoe shook her index finger at me. "We have a deal. No adventures without me."

That gave me an idea. I looked both ways down our street. No one was coming. I reached behind my neck, pulled off my gold chain, and handed it to Zoe. "Here. Keep it safe. In case I get jumped by twins on the way to Elena's dad's office."

Zoe backed away from it, her hands in the air. "No, Arcade. It's not mine. I don't want the responsibility! Last time you took it off, it caught your underwear drawer on fire!"

I put my finger to my lips. "Shhhh! You want the whole

world to hear that? It's going to be fine. It's not heating up anymore."

Doug laughed. "Yeah, now it's just a big disco light."

I shoved past them and put my key in the door. "Just hide it under your pillow or something. I'm the only one who can remove the token from the chain anyway. Plus, I don't want Elena the stalker to find out about it. It's safer here."

Zoe put down her backpack and took the chain. She held it up. The Triple T Token spun around and around. "It's such an interesting pattern on the front. Three Ts. I can't help but wonder if the artist had something else in mind when he crafted his design. See how they're connected?" She ran her fingers over the tops of the Ts. "They look like arches, but without the curve."

"I've wondered the same thing too. That's why I have to get back to that boy."

"Do you really think he's the maker of the mold?"

I shrugged. "That's what Ruah said. And the sign did say GET TRUTH."

"Well then guess what, Arcade," Doug said, slinging his arm over my shoulder, "We need to GET SOME MORE TRUTH."

I ran most of the way to 575 Columbus Avenue, keeping an eye out for twins. Young *and* old. When I arrived in front of the office building at three forty-five, Elena Salvador Castro was waiting for me.

No surprise there.

"Hello, Livingston!" Elena smirked as she leaned against a pillar with her arms crossed. "I figured there was a fifty-fifty chance of you actually showing."

"Ah, well, if you *really* knew me, you'd know that I keep my word. Even when I'm being blackmailed."

"Guess I should get to know you better, then." She smiled and stood up straight.

I held my hands out and waved them around. "WAIT! NO! LOOK OUT!!!" I covered my head with my hands.

Elena dropped to the ground and put her hands over her head. "What?"

I laughed. "Never mind. I just thought you were holding up the building, being a super athlete and all."

Elena fake-laughed. "You're a funny kid, Livingston. Let's go get you some new glasses." She held the door open for me.

"Oh, no. Ladies first." I grabbed the door handle and ushered her in.

We walked toward the elevator.

This is going to be weird. No chain. No token. Normal elevator.

Elena poked the up button, and a door immediately opened.

It was empty.

Yep. This is going to be super weird.

I gestured toward the elevator. "Ladies first."

She smiled. "Thank you."

We both walked in and the door closed.

I inhaled, getting ready to ask Elena about the Greece books, but she started in with her own speech first.

"Now, Livingston, I just want to get couple of things straight! I'm not as bad a person as you think I am. I just want to help people. It's how God made me and I think that's why I want to be a missionary, or an eye doctor, or both. And even though I'm strong and athletic, I'm NOT a bully and I DON'T think I'm ALL THAT, and it was just an ACCIDENT that I broke your glasses, so it's not fair that you won't let me replace them because that's what decent and honest people do. So *you* really put me up to the stalking, you know, which I also don't do, but you gave me no choice, and even though I baked you cookies and gave you movie tickets and cinnamon rolls and socks and books, I need you to know one VERY IMPORTANT THING . . ."

I was in a daze by now.

"W-wh-wha-what?"

Elena stepped back from me, took a deep breath, and let it out.

"No matter what it looks like, I DON'T want to be your girlfriend." Then she made a motion with her hands, like an umpire does when he calls someone safe at home.

I just stood there.

"WELL? Aren't you going to say something?" The light from the elevator danced in her eyes. I couldn't bring myself to say a thing, because what she just said was . . . SO HILARIOUS.

All I could do was laugh. The doubled-over,

can't-breathe, eyes-watering, snot-comes-out-your-nose kind of laugh.

"Hahahahahahahaha! My *girlfriend*? HAHAHAHAHAHA! I nev . . . I mean, I can't believe you would think that I would think . . . oh, hahahahahahaha . . ." I looked up at her. "Do you have a tissue?"

Elena Salvador Castro *wasn't* laughing. She reached into her crossbody bag and pulled out a fast food napkin. "You're killing me, Livingston."

I breathed in and out, trying to calm myself down. I tried to talk again. "Boy, my stomach muscles hurt. I haven't laughed that hard in a long time." I pulled my glasses off my face and wiped the tears off them with the napkin. "Thanks for . . . thanks for setting me straight there. I've been . . . losing sleep over that one."

Elena narrowed her eyes at me. "You're a funny boy, Livingston." Then she smiled. "Would you like to be friends?" She held out her hand to shake mine.

"Um, well . . . huh? Okay. Sure. I guess."

She smiled even bigger. "Good. Glad we got that straight."

It took forever for the elevator to reach the twenty-third floor.

Ding!

The door slid open and I followed Elena down the hallway.

"Hey, Elena, we had a deal! You were going to tell me how you knew about the Greece books."

She glanced over at me. "Sure. As soon as you're finished with the appointment and your new glasses are ordered. But I assure you, it wasn't hard to figure out."

We opened the glass door that said James Castro, OD. A smiling receptionist greeted us. "Elena, great to see you, as always!" Then she looked at me. "And you must be Arcade Livingston."

"Yes, ma'am."

She typed something into her computer. "Right on time. Your parents just emailed over their consent to treat you, so you can go on back. Elena knows the way. Exam room two."

"How did my parents know about this?" I asked Elena.

"I got their number from someone and asked the office to call them. Remember, you caused me to have to stalk you."

"Okay. It's my fault. I get it."

Elena stopped. "Wow. You're seeing things more clearly already." She led me to a chair in an open room. "Your eye chart awaits."

Whenever I go to the eye doctor, I feel like I'm about to fail a test. When you have 20/400 vision, you have no chance. No chance at all.

I sat down on the chair. Elena handed me a gray piece of plastic with a flat round end. "Keeping your glasses on, cover your left eye with this, and read the smallest line you can on the chart, please."

"I thought my appointment was with your dad." I put the plastic over my left eye.

"He'll be here in a minute. I'm sort of in training. Plus, we're friends now, so you're helping me."

"Oh, I see."

"Which line?"

"No, I meant, I understand."

"Oh. What line do you see best?"

I shrugged. "The bottom line, of course."

"Really?" Elena looked at my glasses up close. "Go on . . ."

"Okay, the first letter is a . . . hmmm . . . yeah. I'm sure it's an A."

Elena jumped back. "What? You can see that? I'm so surprised!"

Got lucky on that one.

"And then there's an E . . . no wait, it's an R. Yes, definitely an R."

"Uh . . ."

"Followed by a C, an A, a D, and an E! Hey, Elena, did you know that the bottom line of your dad's eye chart spells ARCADE?"

Elena grabbed the plastic piece from me. "It does not! You're such a—"

"Arcade Livingston! Welcome to Castro Optometry." A nice-looking, middle-aged man stood at the entrance to the room, holding a file folder. He extended his hand. "I'm Dr. Castro. I hear my daughter ruined your glasses."

"Actually, a volleyball did, sir."

He nodded. "Ah, yes, well, we have a lot of that going on around here. We're happy to replace them for you." He took the glasses off my face and took a wet wipe to them. Then he squinted through them. "How long have you had these glasses, Arcade?"

"Got 'em when I started fifth grade . . . no wait. Fourth grade. I remember because I wanted them to match my backpack, which was red at the time."

"So, three years? You know that your eyes can change quite a bit at your age? We may have to make some adjustments to your prescription." Dr. Castro swung the big, gray "seeing eye" machine—that's what I call it, at least— over in front of me. The one with all the lenses that they flip back and forth to see which one works best for you.

"Elena, can you help CiCi at the desk? She's a little behind with recordkeeping."

Elena popped up from the stool in the corner. "Sure, Dad." And then she was gone.

Dr. Castro winked at me. "You can relax now. She means well, but she can be a little intense. My job is to make sure you *pass* the eye exam."

After a few minutes of me choosing lens one instead of two, and three instead of four, and not being able to decide between four and five, Dr. Castro pulled the seeing eye machine away. He turned on the light, sat across from me on his stool, and crossed his arms.

"I've got some great news for you, Arcade. Your eyes haven't changed at all."

"Not at all?"

"No. Same prescription as your current glasses."

"But I've been having trouble reading . . . some things."

"Really? Hmmm. Have you been under any extra stress lately?"

Ya think?

"Just all the normal middle-school stress."

"Have you been straining your eyes with too much late-night reading or computer usage?"

Or laser beams from a golden arcade token, blinding me temporarily?

"Nothing . . . out of the ordinary . . . for me."

Dr. Castro flipped his file shut. "Okay then. We'll blame puberty."

"As long as we keep that between us, it's fine with me."

Dr. Castro laughed. "You want these same frames? I think we have them in stock here. Or you can order a different style to match your backpack."

I stood up. "Which is black with pink flamingos. Probably best I stick with red."

Dr. Castro nodded. "Well, that will speed things up quite a bit. I'll put in a rush order and they should be ready by Monday or Tuesday."

"Thank you, sir."

"And if you take these glasses to Glenda in our fitting department, she'll be able to fix them up with some glue and clear tape so they don't look so . . ."

"Ridiculous?"

"Glasses are never ridiculous, Arcade. I was going to say broken. So they don't look so broken." He handed them back to me. "Ask Elena to show you where to go."

"I will." I turned to leave.

"Arcade? I just have to say ..." Dr. Castro started to laugh. "That was a *great* joke you played on my daughter.

I'm going to change row six on my chart to say ARCADE.
Elena's due for her eye exam soon."

I smiled. "That would be sweet!"

What a cool guy!

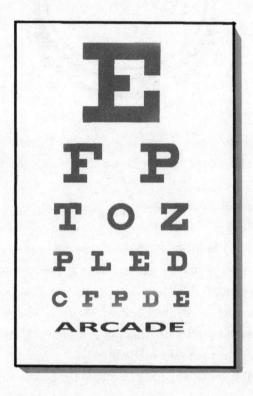

My friend Chondra works at the school library. She told me you were looking for books about Greece. There. Are you satisfied?"

"That's it? That's how you knew what books I wanted? I don't believe you. There has to be more."

Elena and I walked down the hall to the large room where everyone goes to pick out glasses frames and get them fitted.

"Why should there be more? I ordered the books online, got them same-day delivery, and left them on your doorstep."

"How did you know which ones to order? I never told Chondra that I wanted specific titles."

"Well that was as random as could be. I chose the first three that popped up that I could get same-day. Are they books that will be helpful in your research?"

The books! Where are they? Oh, no!

I had been so distracted by the conversation with Ruah that I left them in the hotel room in Reykjavík!

"Oh, um . . . the books? Yes, they were perfect."

We entered the room and I put my name down on

the list to be seen by Glenda. Then we wandered around, looking at all the new frame styles. But Elena wouldn't get off the subject of the books.

"They were perfect, huh? How so? Did you read them already? I know you're a big reader."

I walked from case to case, trying on new frames and checking myself out in the mirror. I tried on a pair of white square frames. "What do you think of these?"

"Which book was the most helpful, Arcade? C'mon, tell me."

I pulled the frames off my face. "I can't."

"Why not?"

"Because I . . . lost them."

Elena's mouth dropped open. "You LOST them? Whoa, it's a good thing they weren't library books! How does a booklover lose books! That's unheard of!"

"Oh, I'm getting quite good at it these days. Between Doug and my sister . . ."

"You're not going to blame your brother and Zoe, are you?"

"How do you know my sister's name?"

Elena put a hand up. "Stalker."

"You're pretty good at that. Have you thought of going into detective work when you grow up?"

"No, I told you, I'm going to be a missionary. Or an eye doctor. Or a mixture of the two. I like the thought of helping people see."

"So you're a Christian? Me too."

"Yeah, I am. And I can't think of *anything* more exciting

that going to other parts of the world to tell people how wide, how long, how high, and how deep God's love for them really is."

I almost dropped the funny white frames. "WHAT did you just say?"

Elena stepped back and crossed her arms "You really need to listen better, Livingston! I was talking about the love of *God*. If people really knew the truth about His love, then they'd know the truth about themselves, and that would make all the difference in the way they live."

"What? What truth about themselves?"

"Arcade Livingston?" Glenda had walked over to where we stood by the glasses case. "Looks like you have some frames that need patching up. Come with me."

Elena smiled and waved as I walked off with Glenda. Then she checked her phone. "Oops, gotta go, Livingston. I'll see you at school."

"Wait! Where are you going?"

She gave me a funny look. "Not telling. If you want to find out, you'll just have to stalk me. And I'm much harder to follow than you are." She laughed, turned, and disappeared down the hallway.

Just like Ruah!

Glenda held a pair of frames that were exactly like my current broken ones. "Come on over, and we'll get these fitted for you. I'm sure you are looking forward to seeing things more clearly."

In more ways than one.

CHAPTER 20
O Mortal

I had a hard time sleeping that night. The truth . . . the truth . . . gotta find the truth . . . yawn . . .

I got up and searched my bookshelf for my Bible. It was hard to find in the midst of all the books about the Amazon River, Iceland, and Greece. Oh, I found it! In the middle of the bookends Mom and Dad bought me.

I opened up to the center. Book of Proverbs.

I squinted and held the book closer. I held the book further back. NO! This can't be happening! I . . . CAN'T . . . SEE!

"AAAAAAAAHHHHHHHHHH!"

"ARCADE! Would you mind? I'm trying to sleep here!"

I was shaking. No, someone was shaking me.

"Arcade! You're having a nightmare."

I jolted and sat up in my bed. "Huh? Doug? What are you doing here?"

"I live here! And I'm trying to sleep here too. You're making it hard with all your screaming."

I jumped out of bed and turned on the light.

Doug covered his eyes. "Aw, no. Why'd you have to go and do that? I'm wide awake now."

I fumbled around for my glasses and went over to my bookshelf, carefully scanning the titles. "Where are all the books about the Amazon, Iceland, and Greece? And *where* is my Bible?"

Doug pulled a Bible out from under his pillow. "I'm sorry. I borrowed it last night. Needed to calm myself about Gram. Is that what the screaming was about?"

"No. I was dreaming that when I opened it, I couldn't see anything written in it."

"You've had that dream before."

"And it's happened in real life now too."

Doug opened the Bible and handed it to me. "Can you read it now? Here, give it a shot."

I dropped my eyes on the page and read the first thing I saw.

"'He has shown you, O mortal, what is good. And what does the Lord require of you? To act justly and to love mercy and to walk humbly with your God.' Hmmm. This is the passage Dad wrote to me on my birthday. Well, close, at least. He mentioned that it's a great passage to ponder."

Doug took the Bible from me and looked at it, scratching his head. "Mortal, huh? Act justly? Love mercy? I hate to say it, bro, but this is way over my head."

"Arcade." A small, tired voice came from the hallway. Zoe was wearing her reindeer onesie, the one with the silly hood, complete with antlers.

"Hey, Rudolph."

She rubbed her eyes. "Don't make fun of me when I'm here to check on you. I heard screaming. Were you reading a scary book?"

"Nah," Doug held the Bible out. "He was trying to read a good book, but he couldn't, and *that* was scary. But he's okay now."

"Oh. Is that all? Well, can you keep it down? I'm tired, and my circadian rhythm is off since our long day in Iceland. Maybe that's why you're having trouble with your eyes, Arcade. Every time we go through those doors, it's like we're living in another time zone, and then we come back here, and no time has passed. Our rhythms are fried."

"No, that's not what it is, Zoe. Dr. Castro said my prescription hasn't changed. It can't be my physical eyes." I took the Bible from Doug and read Dad's verse again. "Walk humbly with my God. I wish I could think like God thinks."

Zoe yawned. "But the Bible says that God's thoughts are higher than ours. So how can it be possible to think his thoughts?" She stood and walked toward the door.

"That's it! I gotta go somewhere *high*! That's what Ruah said! And you know what? Elena mentioned it too!"

"The volleyball villain?"

"Yes! And I'm starting to believe what she said is true. It's no accident that volleyball hit me in the face."

It was three o'clock in the morning in the dead of winter, but when I said that, Triple T lit the place up. Light beams swirled on the walls and ceiling.

"I knew I shouldn't have worn my onesie."

"I could have told you that!" I laughed and watched as golden doors slid down from my ceiling.

I put my arm around my tired friend. "Doug, you can sit this one out if you want."

He grabbed his pillow off his bed. "Are you kiddin'? Why would I ever do that?"

We all watched as the coin slot appeared, like a golden branch growing up through the floor. A little plaque in the shape of a leaf dangled from the bottom that said GET TRUTH.

I tugged gently, and the token fell right off the chain into my hand. "I'd like to go to the high-EST place, please." I dropped the token into the pulsing slot.

Doug ran to his bed and grabbed a small blanket this time. "Really, Arcade? Did you have to pick the *highest* place? You know where that is, *don't you?*"

"Yes, and it's cold." I turned to Zoe. "Guess the onesie was a good choice after all."

The elevator doors rolled open, and Zoe and I stepped in. Doug stood outside the elevator, gripping the pillow and blanket like life preservers.

"It'll be okay, Doug. We always make it back."

"There's also not a lot of oxygen up there."

"There wasn't any oxygen on the moon when we went."

"He's got a point." Zoe pulled her antler hood up.

I tried not to laugh at the antlers sticking a foot above her head. "Hey, are you admitting that I'm right?"

"No! I just said you have a point. Right on the top of your head."

I reached over and flicked one of her antlers. The doors began to close.

"Doug, you comin'?"

His eyes got big, and he ran to the bunks and snatched *my* pillow. "Arcade, why you gotta do this to me?" He dove into the elevator just as the doors closed.

"You know, it may not take us where you think, Doug."

"Oh, I'm *sure* it will." Doug scrunched down in the corner of the elevator, hugging the pillows and shaking. "It's the one place I remember most from geography class last year."

"Lots of people climb there, Doug," Zoe said. "And most survive. Arriving by elevator should help us."

I grabbed hold of my golden chain.

Where did you go, token? Are you back in the mold? Why don't you go with me on these adventures?

Ding!

Is the boy talking with Ruah? Where is the amphitheater? Will I ever find out?

"Arcade."

Why can't I see? How will I see?

"Arcade."

"What, Zoe?"

"We're here."

CHAPTER 21

High-EST

The doors open. We're on the top of the world. Mount Everest. I've read lots of books about this place.

Zoe rubs her arms. "I'm not cold. How come?"

"Never underestimate the warmth of a reindeer onesie."

"Well, *I'm* cold!" Doug shivers. "I guess pizza-slice pjs are substandard gear for around here. Brrrrrr!"

We step out on the summit and turn around and around. Snow covers the peaks below us, but there is nothing above us because this is *Sagarmatha*—the Peak of Heaven.

"THIS IS DOPE!"

I keep turning, then stop and stare down at my feet. "Hey, Zoe, do you think we're in Nepal or Tibet?"

She pulls her hood tighter over her ears and surveys the land around us. "This looks like Tibetan snow to me."

"Aw, then we must be in Nepal."

"Well, maybe *you're* in Nepal and I'm in Tibet."

"Sounds like truth to me," Doug says. "You two are *always* in different worlds." Doug jumps over to a little snow patch between me and Zoe. "Hey, what if I'm *right on the border*?"

"Then you are in the best of places, Mr. Baker. From there you can see both sides of the argument." A woman in a white snowsuit approaches us from the open elevator doors.

Doug points his finger at the woman. "Hey! Are you . . ."

Ruah nods. "I am."

Doug comes over and gives me a jumping high five. "I'm so glad I came! I finally saw her. I mean, yeah, I saw her before, at the gold refinery, but I didn't know it was her then."

"I'm glad you came, too, Doug." Just saying that sentence makes me a little short of breath.

"You are in the highest place." Ruah comes over and places her hand on my chest.

"With the lowest amount of oxygen," Zoe puts her hand on my forehead. "No more high fives, Arcade. We have one-third of the breathable oxygen than we have at home."

"We had more air on the moon." Doug tries to suck in a breath.

"Because you had space suits and oxygen tanks." Ruah smiles. "You will be fine," Ruah says to Zoe. "But only for a short time. Humans are not made to exist up here for long. Heights above 26,000 feet cause rapid pulse, poor sleep, loss of appetite, and confused thinking."

"See! I told you heights are bad!" Doug squeezed his pillow.

"No," I say. "They have a purpose. This place is an -EST, right Ruah?"

"It's called Ever-est!" Zoe looks down at the mountain peaks below us. "Is your thinking becoming confused already, Arcade?"

I don't respond to Zoe, but zero in on Ruah. "What's the purpose of a widest, a longest, a highest, a deepest . . . anything? What's the purpose of an -EST, Ruah?"

She smiles, turns, and heads back toward the elevator. "You'll need to ask one to find out." She points a finger at me.

"What? Wait! I have one more question!"

She tilts her head. "Yes?"

"Why is it that you only sometimes show up on these adventures?"

Ruah reaches into her puffy snowsuit pocket and pulls a lump of metal out of her pocket. It's the mold! She takes the top off, revealing the Triple T Token. "Sometimes he's late."

She takes off toward our elevator, walks right through it, and disappears.

"WE'RE ALMOST THERE, SIR! THE SUMMIT! DO NOT GIVE UP HOPE!"

The sound of crunching snow, hard breathing, and axes picking at ice echo below us.

"Arcade! Hide! We'll be seen!" Zoe turns around and around. She grabs me and Doug, but there is nothing up here and nowhere to go.

"Just play it cool." I try to shake Zoe off my sleeve.

"No problem there." Doug shivers and grabs his pillow tighter.

"Act natural, Zoe. Well, as natural as you can in a reindeer onesie." I turn just as the two heavily clothed, weathered climbers reach the summit.

"Never mind. Just freeze." I stand there like a statue.

If we're out here much longer, it will become reality.

"TENZING! TODAY WE HAVE MADE HISTORY!"

They are shocked to see us, of course.

"WHAT IS THIS?!?" The first man grabs his chest. I hope he's not having a heart attack. "Tenzing! I thought we were going to be the FIRST to summit Everest! What has happened!?!"

The other man circles us, throwing his hands up in the air. "WHO ARE YOU PEOPLE?"

He reaches out to poke my arm. "Why aren't you frozen, young man? You are standing there in your pajamas! We *must* be hallucinating, Sir Edmund. No one can withstand the temperatures up here dressed like this!"

Sir Edmund unhooks from his oxygen bottle and walks up to Zoe. "Am I hallucinating about a reindeer? This is NONSENSE!" He smacks one of her antlers.

"Ah . . . ah . . . ah . . . CHOOOOOOO!" Doug sneezes icy gel from his nose and it immediately freezes into a snotberg.

"Do hallucinations sneeze, Tenzing?"

Okay, time to go to plan B.

"Hello, friends! Congratulations on making it to the summit. My name is Arcade Livingston, your welcoming Sherpa."

I had read that the Sherpas who live down below on the mountain really know their way around here.

"I know all the Sherpas," Tenzing says. "And you are NOT one of them."

"He meant yeti." Doug breaks the frozen snot from his nose. "We're yetis. Except the girl. She's, well . . . a reindeer, as you can see."

DOUG!

"What shall we do, Tenzing? It seems we have been beaten to the summit by children. What will we tell the British public?"

"You could call it the Miracle on Everest," I say, and grin. But *they* are not grinning.

Both men are breathing hard now. Sir Edmund falls down in the snow. "I am not feeling well."

Zoe jumps into bossy, big-sister mode. "You have to eat."

"I do not feel like eating. And I do not take commands from reindeer!"

"I hate to admit it, but my sister's right." I step forward to help Sir Edmund up. "You don't feel like eating because you have altitude sickness. But if you don't eat, you'll die. Humans weren't made to survive up here. It's too high."

Tenzing takes what looks like an unwrapped candy bar out of his pack and hands it to Sir Edmund. "Here, try this. Then we must head down. The children are right."

"What time is it?" Sir Edmund takes a bite.

"Eleven-thirty, sir. We must head down."

Edmund finishes the candy bar and brushes the snow off his suit. "Well, then, we shall head down." He comes up close to examine my face. "Clearly, you are a figment of my imagination, or some kind of god, or you would be quite frozen by now. I think it would be honest to claim ourselves as the first mortals to summit the highest place on earth. Do you think we could trouble you to take a picture of us for the British newspaper?"

"It would be an honor, Sir."

He hands me his camera, and I take it with trembling fingers. I've never used an old-fashioned camera before. Or any camera, for that matter, except the one on my phone. I hold it up to my face. There's a little square opening in the top corner, and I look through it, trying to get both the guys in. "Scrunch in closer . . . a little more."

"Just don't step back, or you'll descend much faster than you planned." Doug laughs nervously under his frozen breath.

"Take the picture, Arcade!" Zoe jumps up and down and rubs her arms and legs. Guess the onesie has reached its limit.

"Hang on, I can't focus. There's a strong beam of light in your faces."

Tenzing and Sir Edmund hold their gloved hands up to block the light beams. "Drat that noontime sun!" Sir Edmund steps back. Zoe throws a hand out. "NO! You'll fall off!" She runs toward me, grabs the camera, and pushes me aside. "You and Doug get over by the elevator. Be ready to drop the token in. I'll just be a minute." She points the camera at the two men. "Smile!"

The men hold their hands up in a victory pose.

"Congratulations, Sir Edmund," Tenzing says. "We have made history. The first to summit Everest on May 29th, 1953!"

Zoe smiles and clicks the camera a bunch of times.

Tenzing runs forward. "Stop. How many photos did you take? We need to save film for logging the descent."

"Film?" Zoe hands the camera back. "Oh, yeah. I've heard about that. I only took ten or twelve."

"Ten? Twelve? Heavens, reindeer! Who takes that many pictures of the same thing?"

Zoe laughs. "Everybody I know."

The token's shining so bright the whole peak of the mountain glows. It's beautiful, but I could use a little heat right now because I can barely feel my fingers. I somehow manage to squeeze them together to pull the token off the chain.

"Come on, Dasher! Let's get back to our warm house in New York City!" I walk up to the coin slot, which has that golden sign—GET TRUTH—sitting right above it.

"Maybe the purpose of the highest place is to put me in my proper place."

Walk humbly with my God.

I let go of the token, and the doors open.

Creak!

The heat and light that radiates from the inside of the elevator draws Doug and me right in. The reindeer is not far behind.

"Close, close, close, close, close!" she yells.

"I agree with Zoe!" I can't believe I say that.

And the doors close.

"I love heat." Doug is back in his corner, snuggled under his blanket.

The glow from the golden dome warms our chilled bones. I stare up, wishing I could make out everything the gold plaques say.

"I gotta go to the library tomorrow. Zoe, you need to find those overdue books so I can get my card unblocked."

The golden elevator returned us right back to Doug's and my bedroom. I checked the clock. "Three a.m. Sorry about your circadian rhythm, Zoe, but it was pretty cool to be the first people to scale Everest. It will be our little secret."

Zoe pushed the antlers off her head. "Hey, no picture means it didn't happen."

"And Sir Edmund and Tenzing have twelve." Doug laughed as he climbed up to his bunk.

"No, Doug, we can't sleep yet!" I said.

"We can't sleep yet?"

"No, we can't sleep yet."

"Oh, yeah? Watch me!" Doug rolled onto his bed, shoved his body between the sheets, and threw the comforter over his head.

"Why can't we sleep yet?" Zoe looked ridiculous, standing there, tapping her hoof.

"I need to find the card with Kenwood Badger's phone number on it. I want to contact him."

Zoe held her hands up. "Oh, no. We are NOT going there, Arcade. Those Badger brothers are the meanest, baddest—"

"That's IT! They're -ESTS, too, and I need to find out why. Kenwood wants to make things right. Shouldn't I show him mercy?"

"Like we said before, it could be a setup! Leave it alone, Arcade." Zoe turned to walk out the door.

"Maybe. But I'm going down to the dumpster to find that card."

"You mean PIECES of the card! I ripped that baby up good."

"So I'll be down there awhile. I can't sleep anyway. Circadian rhythm is all messed up."

Doug threw the comforter off and sat up. "Ugh! Mine is too." He jumped down to the floor. "Let's go."

Zoe sighed. "Okay. Let me go change. I'm not pawing around the trash in this."

We changed into our grubby clothes, then tip-toed down the stairs, carefully avoiding stair five, which squeaks if you step right in the middle. Thankfully, Zoe puts a blanket over Milo's cage at night, so we didn't have to hear some awful cockatoo commentary on our way out.

"Hold the door open for me." Zoe grabbed the stepladder from the pantry and brought it out the side kitchen door. "Brrr! What's with the wind?"

"Aw, come on, sis, you've just been to Everest." I reached up and clicked my headlamp on.

We climbed into the small trash dumpster that we share with our neighbors. They must have had a party last night, because we found ourselves swimming in pizza boxes.

"At least it still smells good." Doug sniffed and grabbed his belly.

"Oh, ugh," Zoe groaned. "I think I just stepped in a banana."

"Try to ignore that and look for small pieces of a ripped-up, white index card."

"It's no use, Arcade. We'll never find them." Zoe pulled a brown peel from her foot. "This. Is. Disgusting."

"Hmmmm." I sorted through paper plates, pizza crusts, and red plastic cups. "Zoe, where did you put those pieces when you ripped them up?"

She took a minute to think. "I threw them in the trash in the bottom bathroom."

"You mean the trash I'm supposed to empty twice a week but *always forget*?"

"Yeah."

"CHA-CHING! Let's get outta here!"

Sometimes it pays to forget to do your chores. But not in allowance.

We tried to brush all the trash-stink off outside, but it was no use. As soon as we got in, Loopy came running and attacked us for a lick-fest.

"Loop, hang on, boy, I got papers to find." Doug held Loopy while I retrieved the small trash bag from the bathroom and brought it into the kitchen. I was just about to pour everything out on the dining room table when Zoe stopped me.

"Not so fast!" Zoe went to the pantry and brought out a large plastic trash bag. She spread it on the table. "Now you can dump."

I poured out used tissues, an empty hand soap container, and a broken pencil.

"See? This is why I don't need to empty this twice a week."

There was also a candy bar wrapper, a broken hair tie, and a ball of hair. I picked that up and held it out for Zoe. "This yours?"

"Hey, at least I clean out my brush."

Scattered among those items were little bits of white index card. I picked them out, and Doug and Zoe pieced them together on the table.

"I got the KB!" Doug said. "And a couple of numbers. Zoe, what'd you get?"

"Numbers." She held a couple of pieces up. "How do we know what order they go in?"

"Just put the paper together like a puzzle. Why did you have to rip them up so small, Zoe?"

"So you wouldn't try to put them back together! If I'd known that I would have to do it . . ."

"Here's a couple more." I was handing the pieces to Doug when I heard a car pull into our side drive. "Oh, no! Who's that?"

Zoe peeked through the kitchen window. "It's Dad! Hurry, get all this trash out of here!"

I can't believe we forgot Dad was still at work. He usually gets home around three-thirty. We threw the trash contents back in the little bag. Loopy was chewing on the candy bar wrapper.

"Give me that, Loop!" I pulled it away from him, stuffed it in the trash, and ran the basket back to the bathroom. Zoe gathered up the big trash bag and threw it in the kitchen garbage, and Doug headed for the refrigerator.

Dad opened the side kitchen door and jumped when he found us all waiting for him.

"Well, hello! To what do I owe a greeting from all of my kids this early in the morning?"

Doug stuck his head up over the refrigerator door. "Hey, Mr. L. We couldn't sleep, so we're makin' a snack. You want a quesadilla?" Doug took out some cheese and tortillas and plopped them on the counter.

Dad yawned and stretched. "Sounds tempting, but I'm wiped. How about you make me some pancakes and bacon around noon tomorrow?"

Doug shot an index finger out. "You got it, Mr. L!"

"That will be fabulous. I'll see you all then."

I raised my hand. "I'll have to take a raincheck. I'm going to the library."

Dad put down his bookbag and unbuttoned the top button of his dress shirt. "Tomorrow? I don't think so, bud. Have you watched the news? We've got a nor'easter coming. I don't think anyone in New York City is going anywhere."

"Nor'easter? That's awesome!" Doug pulled a pan from

the cupboard and started making cheese quesadillas. "Too bad tomorrow's not a school day."

"Well, I hope people can get to the show tomorrow night. We'll have to see how much snow this thing dumps. See you all for pancakes!" Dad left his bag on the chair and walked up the stairs.

"Are you gonna put some chilis in those?" I dug in the pantry and pulled out a can. "And how about olives?"

"You got it!"

I got the can opener and started cranking away on the olive can. "Zoe, you want some quesadillas?"

Zoe was searching through the junk drawer of the desk in the corner. "Sure. I'm starving from being the first reindeer to summit Everest." She held up some tape. "Do you have the card pieces? I'll tape them together while you guys cook."

"Sounds good to me." I pulled the pieces from the silverware drawer where I had thrown them before Dad came in. After picking them out from the spoon section, I gave them to Zoe.

"You've being awfully cooperative." I raised an eyebrow.

"Well, maybe I don't want to be the stubborn-est anymore." She frowned. "I wonder if Michael will ever talk to me again."

I flicked her ear. "He will. You annoy people, but you do it in a way that makes them miss you when it's not happening."

Zoe pulled a piece of tape off the dispenser and stuck it

on my nose. "That's the nicest thing you've ever said to me, Arcade."

I gave her a goofy smile. "Nice-EST. That's me."

"Those were some of the best quesadillas I've ever had," Doug announced, using his last tortilla triangle to wipe up the salsa on his plate. "Not sure I can sleep now." He took our plates and rinsed them off in the sink. "You guys want to watch some TV?"

Zoe pushed herself away from the table. "No. It's going to be light soon, and I need to get *some* sleep. I'll see you all later. Don't bug me. *Unless* Triple T wakes up, of course."

"Sure thing," I said. "You're annoying, but we do have a deal."

"Yes, we do." She picked up the taped note from Kenwood Badger. "And I'll just keep this. Don't want you doing anything stupid—"

"Zoe!" I reached for it, but she took off quick. She ran up the stairs and closed her door. Doug shook his head and laughed. "Zoe's the best! Zoe's the best!"

"Thanks for the support, Milo."

CHAPTER 23
Nor'easter

*M*anhattanites should plan to hunker down as the first *nor'easter of the year heads our way. Prepare for snow—lots of it! And that means slow traffic. Authorities recommend staying home if possible, but if you do need to go somewhere in the city—get out those heavy coats and snow boots. Walking will be the fastest way to get anywhere today.*

"Sounds like that's my cue to get in bed and stay there." Doug pulled himself up from the couch, grabbed the remote, and turned off the news. "You comin'?"

"Sure. Guess I have all day tomorrow to figure out how to get that paper out of Zoe's room." I followed Doug up the stairs. After being at the top of Mt. Everest and at the bottom of a garbage dumpster, my soft bed was going to feel good.

A knock sounded at the door. "Arcade? Honey? Are you still sleeping? There's a package for you."

Mom's voice from the hallway jolted me out of my deep sleep. "Mom?" I rubbed my eyes. "Come on in."

Mom cracked the door and peeked in. "Hey, sleepyhead. It's one o'clock. A delivery person just brought a package for you."

"One o'clock? In the afternoon?"

Mom turned on the light. "Yes. You picked a good day to sleep in. The snow's really piling up. Which is why I'm surprised this showed up."

She held out the package. It was from Castro Optometry!

"I can't believe it!" I ripped into the package and, sure enough, it was my new glasses.

Mom smiled. "What kind of coincidence is that? The girl who broke your glasses has a dad who's an optometrist?" She shook her head and picked up my old glasses, examining the cracks and scratches. "You've got some kind of charmed life going on, my son."

I scooted out of my blankets and stood up. I closed my eyes tight, then opened them wide a few times.

Mom laughed. "What are you doing? Eye exercises?"

"Just making sure the sleep is out of them, so when I pop these babies on, I'll appreciate the new clarity. I expect great things from these! Hey, now I can READ ALL DAY!"

Mom shook her head. "Don't you always do that?"

I shrugged. "Well, yeah."

Mom watched as I raised the glasses to my face. I closed my eyes, slid on the earpieces . . . adjusted them on my nose . . .

"Enough with the suspense, Arcade. You can open your eyes now."

I opened. And Mom was gone!

I turned in every direction. "MOM! I can't see you! These glasses are terrible!"

She chuckled and popped her head in from the hallway. "GOTCHA! Now get down here and eat breakfast *and* lunch before it's dinner time, okay?"

"Okay."

But first, I flew to my bookshelves to conduct the ultimate test. I ran my fingers over the spines to find the best title. I stopped, shocked, when I came upon a title that wasn't mine.

"*The Care and Feeding of Today's Cockatoo*? I had no idea this was here." I checked the book next to it. Of course, it was *French Decorating*.

Zoe!

"I don't want to read either one of these!"

I stacked the two books on my desk and ran down to the living room, where everyone was chilling, watching TV.

Dad looked up from reading his newspaper. "Hey, Arcade! Nice to see you got a good day's sleep. Would you like to go shovel off the stairs?"

I pulled open the front door, and a wall of snow fell in.

"Arcade!" Zoe palmed her forehead.

"Why didn't anyone warn me? I guess I better shovel the inside now." I went to the kitchen and found our biggest spatula and bowl. "Anyone want snow cones?" I spooned the icy mess into the bowl.

Doug came over to help with his hands. He looked up at my glasses. "Hey, new specs!" Then he leaned over to whisper, "Did you test them on the Greece book?"

"Oh. Unfortunately, I left those books in . . ." I lowered my voice, "Iceland."

"Oh, man."

"And it looks like I'm not getting to the library today. But, hey, we got the Internet. Maybe I can even search African universities and find Aahir."

Doug frowned. "It's been out all morning. Nor'easter strikes again."

We took our bowl of ice to the kitchen and dumped it in the sink.

"So, you're telling me that I'm stuck here *all day* and I can't find out anything about anything except French decorating and how to care for cockatoos?"

"Well, you know what Aahir said, 'Sometimes life is a mystery, Arcade. A huge, exciting mystery!'"

"Haha. Well, I do have something I can focus on."

"What's that?"

"Getting Kenwood Badger's note out of Zoe's room."

I popped my head out from the kitchen and spotted Zoe lounging on the couch, staring out the window at the stormy weather. "Hey, Doug, will you keep Zoe distracted for a few minutes?"

"You're going to break the 'DON'T YOU EVER EVEN THINK OF GOING IN MY ROOM WITHOUT ASKING' rule?"

"Hey, she took my property without asking. Plus, I'm

not going to go into her private business, I'm just going to scan the tops of her furniture. If it's just sitting there, I'll snatch it."

"Okay, will you give me a sign when the coast is clear?" Doug wrung his hands and peeked around the corner at Zoe.

"Sure. I'll, uh . . . I'll come downstairs."

"Okay, I'll keep the Zoe-girl engaged. Just make it quick."

"Will do." I held out my fist, and Doug bumped it.

"Be careful. If she catches you, you're dead."

I strolled out to the living room. "I'm gonna go get dressed."

Zoe glanced over. "It's about time, slacker."

Bawk! Zoe's always right! Zoe's always right!

"I'm also going to go read about the life expectancy of cockatoos. Your overdue library books are on *my* bookshelf!"

"Oh, is *that* where they are? See, I told you it wasn't my fault. You probably took them so you could read them—"

"Why would I want to read a book about your annoying bird?"

Zoe rolled her eyes and lay back on the couch. "Just go get dressed."

I ran up the stairs and crept slowly down the hallway. I stopped at Zoe's door and listened for the sound of any person who might be climbing the stairs behind me. Nothing. Instead I heard Doug.

"Hey, Zoe, can you explain to me how you fixed the fondant mistake I made on Arcade's cake? If I'm going to open a bakery, I need to know how that stuff works."

"Sure, Doug . . ."

I wiped the sweat from my palms on my pajama pants. I reached for the knob . . .

Woof!

"Loop!" I pushed him away. "This is not a good time."

I turned the knob slowly and pushed the door open . . . just a crack. I scanned the floor. Nothing. Scanned the bed. Nothing. Scanned the desk. Nothing.

Then . . . I spotted it! It was on her nightstand. I could see a corner of it sticking out from under a tissue box.

Good thing I got these new glasses.

I took a deep breath and went in. Took three huge steps, grabbed the card, and took two larger steps out. Five steps hardly count for GOING IN MY ROOM WITHOUT ASKING.

I closed the door behind me and slumped to the floor. "We made it Loop. Loop?" I heard scratching from the other side of the Zoe's door.

Oh, no!

I opened her door again, grabbed Loopy, and dragged him out. I carried him and the notecard into my room and closed the door. "Loopy, you almost got me into real trouble just now."

I put him down on the bed, sat down next to him, and read the card.

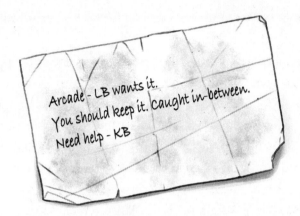

Arcade - LB wants it.
You should keep it. Caught in-between.
Need help - KB

Below the note was the phone number. I grabbed my phone out of my backpack and added Kenwood Badger to my contacts.

Now if I return this to Zoe's room, she won't suspect anything.

"Loopy, stay right here." I jumped up off my bed, tiptoed down the hallway, listened for a minute . . .

"So, let me get this straight. You DON'T use a rolling pin?"

"Yes, you do! Doug, are you even listening?"

Good, they're still talking.

I turned the knob, leapt in, this time making it to her nightstand in two and a half steps. I positioned the card exactly how I had found it. Then I took two leaps back, got out the door, and slumped to the floor.

"What are you doing down there?"

It was mom. She had some books in her hands.

"Oh, hey, Mom. I was playing with Loopy and he . . . got away."

Mom looked inside my room. "He's here on your bed. On your pillow, to be exact."

I jumped up and ran in my room. "Seriously, Loopy? Get your own pillow." I shooed him off and then walked over to my bookshelves, where Mom was adding some titles.

"I was going through some boxes in my bedroom and found a few of my favorite travel books. I thought you could put them with your new Greece books." She moved a few things around. "Where are those books?"

"Oh, they're still in the box. I'll get to them soon."

The next time I travel to Iceland.

"Okay, well, I'll leave some room up here on the shelf for them." She put the books in between my new bookends. "I also found my old travel journal. You might want to check it out someday when you're bored." She slid a tattered, spiralbound notebook in with the books. "There you go. Happy travels!" She disappeared into the hallway.

Happy travels.

Most of the trips through the elevator doors had been happy. Some had been confusing. And a couple . . . downright scary! Like that trip to San Francisco in 1935, when the Badger brothers hitched a ride, tried to take the token from me, and went plunging over the edge of the unfinished Golden Gate Bridge.

I shivered.

Don't want to do that ever again.

But there was one thing I *did* need to do. I needed to call Kenwood Badger.

CHAPTER 24
Why'd you Do It?

My fingers shook as I entered the password to unlock my phone. I pulled up Kenwood Badger's number and held my index finger over the send button.

What am I gonna say? It could be a setup.

Milo's bird words echoed in my brain.

Zoe's always right! Zoe's always right!

"She is *not*. But either way, this has to end."

I pushed send before I had a chance to chicken out. The phone rang on the other end . . . once, twice, three times. I almost pressed END, but then . . .

"Hello?"

Gulp.

"Hello?" I barely squeaked out.

"Hey, is this you, kid? Arcade Livingston?"

"Uh, yeah. It's me."

"So you got my note?"

"Uh-huh. I'm sorry I didn't call earlier, it's just that—"

"You don't trust me? Hey, I don't expect you to. I knew it was a long shot, but I wanted a chance to thank you."

"Thank me?"

There was silence on the other end, and then a long sigh.

"Yes. I want to thank you for fixing up the windmill course. I know you were the brains behind it. And I just want to know one thing."

My fingers stopped trembling.

"What's that?"

"Why'd you do it?"

I had to dig deep to answer that. I thought back to my trip to India, where my friends and I were blessed by the generosity and hospitality of people we didn't even know. And then there was that clue I found in the journey box: *Where generosity goes, refreshment flows.*

"It was the right thing to do. Forest Games and Golf brings happiness to lots of people."

"The windmill fell down the day my wife died. Did you know that?"

"No. I'm so sorry."

"It was the worst day of my life."

"I'm sure it was."

"After that, Lenwood and I argued all the time. It was all my fault. I couldn't get my head back in the business, and all he wanted to do was expand. He kept talking about how that token was going to make us rich . . ."

"Rich? I don't think that's what the token's for—"

"And all *I* could think of was what good would more money be when I'd just lost the most valuable thing in my life?"

"I . . . I'm so sorry."

"Then one day, after we had another huge blowout, I

took the token, stuffed it in a gold prize container, and hid it in the claw machine! I just wanted to get rid of it and figured NO ONE would find it in there! Have you ever seen anyone pull something that small from a claw machine?"

Never. Well, until my dad did it.

"And then along came your parents, and they have some kind of special love chemistry, and your dad pulls it out. First try! And as soon as that happens, the place goes wild, lights are flashing—"

"Wow."

"And everything went downhill. Equipment started breaking, and our bank account dwindled, so we couldn't fix things. Customers stopped coming. And since it all happened after we lost the token, Lenwood was convinced that it was the token that had caused our success in the first place."

"I . . . don't think that's how the token works."

Kenwood chuckled. "I know that *now*. But I didn't realize it until I got back from San Francisco and saw the windmill upright, the bridge fixed, and that waterfall flowing again. The place was swarming with kids, and business has been booming ever since, *without* us having the token!"

"How did you know I was the one who fixed your course?"

"Gertrude."

"Miss Gertrude ratted us out?"

"Yeah, and then she chewed us out! She always told us the token didn't belong to us, and she was scared we were going to try to hurt your parents when they had it. So, on the day you were born, she just happened to be working at the hospital . . ."

So that's why Miss Gertrude stole the token on my birthday.

". . . and now *you* have the token. But it's different with you. You're doing good things with it. What's different about you, Arcade Livingston? I need to know the truth about you."

"ARCADE!" Zoe yelled from the hallway. "HOW MANY TIMES A WEEK DO I TELL YOU NOT TO GO IN MY ROOM?"

I pushed END on the call and jumped in my bed. Closed my eyes to pretend I was resting. Doug busted in.

"Dude, what happened? You never came down! I can only talk about fondant for so long."

Zoe barged in after Doug. "I see big footprint indentations on my carpet, Arcade!" She pulled back my covers and spotted my phone in my hand. "You *called* him?"

I sat up. "Yeah. I had to."

Zoe threw up her hands. "GREAT! Now he has your number."

"He's been on our *doorstep*, Zoe! He knows everything about us. And I really don't think it's a setup."

My phone rang. "It's him."

"Don't answer it."

I not only answered it, I put it on speaker. Kenwood Badger started talking right away.

"I'm sorry if I scared you. Lenwood and I will be in New York City for an arcade convention on February twenty-second. Meet us at the Bow Bridge in Central Park on the twenty-third, at four o'clock sharp. I have a plan to convince my brother that you're the one who's supposed to have the token."

He hung up.

Zoe slumped down on my desk chair. Doug plopped down on the floor. He looked up at our wall calendar. "We got three weeks. What're you gonna do, Arcade?"

"I'm gonna meet him at the Bow Bridge at four o'clock sharp on February twenty-third."

Zoe stared me down. "How do you know he's telling the truth?"

I pulled my token out from under my pajama shirt. "I don't. But this dazzling truth detector does."

CHAPTER 25

Arcadia

The token broke out in light swirls that projected on the ceiling, the walls, and the floor.

"Yes!" Doug pumped his fist in the air. "We've already been as high as we can go and I survived. I'm ready for anything now."

Zoe laughed. "Maybe the truth about you is you're not really afraid of heights, Doug."

"I've been afraid of heights my whole life." Doug put a finger to his chin. "Huh."

I ran to the closet and put on some jeans, a long-sleeved red T-shirt, and a gray hoodie. Threw on some shoes too. No socks. I didn't need to turn the light on in the closet. The token lit the place up like a bright, summer day.

I took my new glasses off my face and blew the dust from the lenses.

Okay, Elena, I'm ready to see.

Light prisms swirled just like the snow outside, and soon they all clustered in the middle of the room, forming a large rectangle which solidified into golden elevator doors.

"Never gets old, man." Doug stepped forward and placed his hands on the doors. "Where we gonna get truth today?" He pointed to the golden coin slot that jutted out from the middle of the doors. The sign that said GET TRUTH hung in midair right above it.

"Be careful with your request, Arcade." Zoe reached out a finger and traced the word TRUTH on the sign.

"Zoe, by now you should trust me." I reached for Triple T and pulled gently on it, releasing it from its chain. "I want to go back to the kid. The one who made the mold. I think we're connected. Please show me how."

Then I dropped the token. Into the slot, and . . . into the mold?

The elevator doors opened at my command. When we stepped in, I noticed something different right away. The gold walls shined brighter than ever! I tilted my head back to gaze at the dome.

"Zoe! The signs! I can read them!" I squinted. "Well, at least a couple of them."

"No way, Arcade. No one can see that far away."

"Oh, yeah? Well here's what that one says." I pointed up and began to read. "As one lamp lights another, nor grows less, so nobleness enkindleth nobleness."

"Are you making that up? Wasn't that on Miss Gertrude's birthday card?" Zoe had one hand on her hip.

"NO! I don't talk like that, Zoe! 'Nobleness enkindleth nobleness?' What does that even mean?"

"Well, think about the first part. A lamp lights another lamp, but it doesn't go dim itself, right? It works the same way with a noble person. They encourage others to be noble, and on and on it goes. Everything and everyone become brighter."

Doug scratched his head. "Why doesn't it just say *that*? And what is nobleness, exactly?"

"Having or showing qualities of high moral character. Courage, generosity, honor. Stuff like that."

"See, Doug, my older sister's a walking dictionary. She comes in handy sometimes."

Zoe gave me a playful shove. "You wouldn't survive in the world without me and you know it."

I ignored her and kept staring. "I don't *get* it! I couldn't read that sign before. And Dr. Castro said my prescription hasn't changed."

"Well, *something* changed," Zoe said.

DING!

The doors open up to a landscape of green grass and blue sky. A large, lone rock sits in the middle of it all. A boy leans on the rock with his back to us, his shoulders hunched. He looks like he's praying or something.

I put my fingers to my lips, and we step out. Doug rubs his arms and whispers, "Are we invisible?"

I shrug.

Zoe links her arm in mine. As we inch toward the boy, we step carefully through the grass so we don't startle him.

I decide to test things. "Hello?" I say in a quiet voice.

Nothing.

"Hello?" I say a little louder. Still no response.

We keep walking, until we're within a foot of the rock. By now he should almost feel our breath on his neck. He looks up to the sky and starts talking.

"I wish I could play and discover what's out there, beyond the arcades." He shakes his head. "And while I know that is not my lot, I do wish it for someone . . . whoever receives the coin from this mold. I wish that they will imagine possibilities, that they will experience the best adventures that life has to offer. And that they would share what they learn with others."

We stand like statues and watch in awe as a young version of Ruah, wearing a white sweat suit and glittery ballcap, appears before the boy!

The boy jumps. "Who are you?" He looks left, right. "Where did you come from?"

Ruah smiles in her mysterious way. "I came from *you*."

"From *me*?"

"Yes. I am the spirit of your wish."

My mouth drops open. I want to see the boy's face, but I don't dare move.

He stands up from the rock. "I have spent all my childhood years working with my father. But I know there is a world out there full of adventure and learning! I want to know what's out there! Will I *ever* know? I have so many questions." He opens his hands to reveal the mold.

Ruah reaches out. "Will you trust me with this? I will find someone who has the same heart as you. One who can answer your questions."

He hesitates for a moment, but then passes the mold to her. "Really? Is it possible that there is someone out there just like me?"

Ruah clasps her hands around the mold. "I am certain. It will take much travel, difficult testing, and searching for truth. But I promise, I'll find him."

My head feels light, and I stumble back a few steps.

"Arcade, are you okay?" Zoe grabs on tight to my elbow.

I nod, move in closer, and focus my eyes on Ruah. She opens the mold to reveal . . . the Triple T Token!

The boy gasps. "Where did *that* come from?"

Ruah puts her hand on his shoulder. "Pure gold."

"Pure? But that's impossib—"

"*Nothing* is impossible with a wish as strong as yours. I will see you again soon, Theo Timon Theros."

Ruah turns, walks a few feet, and disappears.

Theo Timon Theros. Triple T!

The boy runs forward and waves his hands in the air in front of himself, as if he is searching for the secret door that Ruah has just walked through. He turns in a circle but doesn't see us.

But I get to see his face. And it's glowing.

Then he runs, with energy in his steps, toward a cluster of homes down the hill. In the distance I spot an amphitheater that looks over a crystal blue ocean.

I open my mouth to say something to Zoe, but Ruah appears in front of me. She opens the mold. "Arcade, it is time to go home and experience more adventures. For

Theo, for your friends, and for you." She places the token in my shaking hand.

"So, *I'm* the one that's just like him?"

She places a hand on my heart. "Nobleness enkindleth nobleness."

Ruah waves a hand in the air, and huge light beams shoot out from the token. But this time, before the doors and the coin slot show up, a golden plaque appears on the rock.

Thanks for visiting Arcadia, Greece.

Come back soon!

Inside the elevator, my heart races. "Zoe, do you think I'm the one?"

Zoe doesn't answer.

Doug does.

"Dude, ya think?"

Thanks for visiting
Arcadia Greece.
Come back soon!

CHAPTER 26
The One

Mr. Dooley has tons of energy, which equals extra volume . . . especially on Monday mornings.

"WASN'T THAT A GREAT NOR'EASTER? I BET YOU HOPED THEY WOULDN'T GET THE ROADS CLEARED THIS MORNING, YET HERE YOU ARE—EXCITED AND READY TO FINISH YOUR TIME TRAVEL ASSIGNMENTS!"

My friend Thomas Scranton, who I call Scratchy, turned around in his chair to talk to me in the back row. "You should read my paper, Arcade. It's RAD!" He scratched the back of his neck. "I wrote it like a *what if* story. What if we could travel to the future? Could we find out what the best job would be for us?" He whispered to me behind his hand, "I know I did . . ."

Scratchy had been on a couple of trips with the token. Once we ended up on a pit crew at a NASCAR race, and another time we were stuck in a small plane above New York City—with no pilot!

Carlos leaned in. "Hey, and *what if* we could travel

to the past?" He nudged me with his elbow. "Some of us would learn to appreciate all we have at that moment. I know I did."

Doug chimed in. "And *what if* time travel could teach us more about our true selves? Like, I'm not even sure I was ever afraid of heights now. I think I've been afraid of something else . . ."

"What, Doug?"

"MR. LIVINGSTON, YOU HAVE A VISITOR IN THE HALLWAY."

I scooted back in my chair and stood. I looked out the small window in the classroom door to see the top of a brunette head.

Seriously, Elena?

I straightened my new glasses and walked toward the door.

"Five minutes." Mr. Dooley held out an open hand.

I walked out.

Elena Salvador Castro turned around. "Livingston! Hey, just wanted to make sure you got your glasses. With the nor'easter, I wasn't sure if the delivery would arrive."

"How can you just walk around the hallways during school?"

She laughed. "I'm student body president. It's my job to check on the wellbeing of students in this school." She held out a card. "I have a permanent hall pass." She stepped in close. "So how are those glasses working?"

"They're phenomenal. Did you sprinkle them with pixie dust or something?"

"Pixie dust?"

"Yeah, it has to be magic. I see things I never saw before."

She tilted her head. "That's what all my dad's patients say. When you haven't seen clearly for a while, it seems magical. Kids who get glasses for the first time can't believe they can see individual leaves on trees." Elena looked down both sides of the hallway. "I have to get back. But can I ask you something?"

I just stared at her. "Can I say no?"

She laughed again. "Do you want to run for student body president for next year? I'll be moving on to high school, and I want to leave this school better than I found it."

"And you think I'd be good to take over? Why?"

Elena shrugged. "When I was stalking you, I talked to lots of students. They say you're always helping people. Your uncles even told me what a help you've been to them on their school projects."

"My *uncles*?"

"Oh, come on. I know the Tolleys are your uncles. They showed me where you live the other day."

"HAHAHAHAHAHAHAHA! Oh, my, that's a GOOD one!"

Elena crossed her arms. "WHAT is so funny, Livingston?"

"I guess you're not that great a stalker after all! The Tolleys aren't my uncles. But they do LOVE to mess with people."

"What?!?" She walked up to the classroom window and glared in. "I'll deal with them later. But hey, even Wiley

Overton thinks you're kind of okay, and Wiley's the meanest kid around."

"Maybe he's the meanest because people have been making fun of him his whole life. -ESTS don't just happen by accident, you know."

"-ESTS?"

"Never mind. There's a reason he's like that, Elena."

Elena looked up toward the ceiling and grinned. "You know what, I agree with you. But I still think you're a funny boy, Livingston." She fanned herself with her hall pass. "Give it some thought and let me know. The election's in March. If you're voted in, you'll work with me for a couple of months to get ready for the changeover."

"With *you*? I don't know about that."

She pushed me in the chest. "Oh, come on. You do too know."

I stepped back. "I'll give it some thought."

She headed down the hallway a few steps, and then turned back.

"Livingston, I think you're the one."

CHAPTER 27
-ESTS

For the next week, I watched for -ESTS at school. Reagan Cooper, the only person I've ever seen stand up to Wiley Overton, was the brave-EST girl I knew. Mr. Dooley had the loud-EST voice. CJ Mendoza, my friend who uses a wheelchair, was the tough-EST kid I'd ever met. Scratchy was the handi-EST. That kid could fix anything! And as much as I tried to avoid her, but couldn't, Elena Salvador Castro had the bright-EST eyes I've ever seen. They seemed to flicker with excitement over the most ridiculous things—like me running for student body president.

"Arcade for President," I heard a couple of girls say when Doug and I walked by them after school one day. They giggled and ran away.

"So, I hear you're running for student body president." Doug ribbed me as we walked home through the park the next Thursday afternoon. "You got my vote."

"Doug, I can't run."

"You can't run?"

"That's what I said."

"Why not?"

"Really? Let's count the reasons. I have *Triple T* to figure out. I've got *Badgers* to figure out. Plus, it's a lot of responsibility to take care of all the students at a middle school. Too much pressure."

We took the 86th Street exit, crossed over to the West Side, and headed north toward 88th. Zoe caught up to us at the subway exit.

"Hey, Zoe, you think Arcade would make a good student body president?" asked Doug.

She stopped in her tracks. "Uh . . . NO."

I turned to face her. "No? What do you mean, no?"

"Oh, COME ON, Arcade. You? In politics? You'll confuse everyone with your outside-the-box ideas."

"There's a lot more room to breathe outside the box, Zoe. You should try it sometime."

She smirked. "And where would it end? With you running New York City someday? Lord, help us! With you in charge, we'd end up with ten-sided stop signs on all the street corners."

"We ALREADY HAVE ten-sided stop signs. How many times do we have to debate that? Eight around the outside, *plus* the front and the back. TEN!" I traced an octagon in the air and then clapped my hands together in front of her face.

"Maybe the pressure *would* be too much, Arcade." Doug laughed.

"Pressure?" Zoe tightened her backpack straps. "You guys won't know real pressure until you get to high school."

Doug's phone rang, and he pulled it out of his pocket. "Uh-oh. It's my social worker."

We all stopped.

Doug held his phone up so we could see the screen. "What should I do?"

"Maybe it's good news, Doug," I said. "Answer it."

"Hello? Yeah, this is me . . . uh-huh . . . I understand . . . do we have to do it tomorrow? . . . Yeah . . . okay. I'll be there."

He hung up. "Four o'clock tomorrow. Urgent meeting. I think I'm in deep trouble, Arcade."

CHAPTER 28

Deep-EST

The sidewalk in front of us began to glow, and it wasn't from the late afternoon sun. I pulled Triple T out from under my layers and the place brightened up even more. A hole opened, revealing an illuminated golden staircase that went down, down, down, further than the subway.

"After you guys." I stood back and let Doug and Zoe walk down the stairs in front of me. It took us twenty flights down, but we finally found it. A golden elevator, shaped like a submarine, waited for us at the bottom. It shined so bright we almost couldn't look at it.

"I was hoping to go *up* and test your theory about my fear of heights, Zoe."

"I've never known a submarine to go up, Doug." Zoe ran her hand along the smooth, golden sides of the sub. "It's beautiful."

The words GET TRUTH were carved into the front of the submarine. "It looks like a giant soda bottle laying on its side," I said.

"Never seen a golden soda bottle," Doug said.

"Where's the coin slot?" Zoe pushed her fingers in all the creases she could find, looking for an opening.

I followed the pulsing light coming from the token, all the way to the front of the sub. The nose looked like a giant bottle cap. And it had a slit in it that was pumping out light.

"I think I found it! You guys ready to go deep?"

"If it will get me out of going to the social worker appointment, sure."

"That's never how it works, friend. But maybe we'll learn something that will help you."

I pulled the token off the chain and dropped it into the coin slot. When I did, even more light came pouring out of the slot and out from the walls of the sub. I walked to the middle and pressed my palms together. "Give us some deep truth. Something we can hold onto." I pulled my palms apart, and the sub doors flew open. When we stepped in and the doors closed, the sub tipped!

"Hold on, guys!" I yelled.

But there was nothing to hold on to.

We slid all the way down to the nose of the sub, and we began to drop.

"Look! It's the gold dome!" Zoe stared up from where we had slid. "Why would those signs be up there if we can never see them?"

I tilted my head up and my heart pumped a little harder when I spotted a new plaque I could read!

I adjusted my glasses. "YOU GUYS. I HAVE ONE."

"You have one?" Doug squinted and stood on his tip-toes.

"Yeah! Clear as if it were in my hand."

"Well, what does it say?"

"It says, 'The inquiry, knowledge, and belief of truth is the sovereign good of human nature.'"

Zoe jostled me with her elbow. "There's NO WAY you can see that, Arcade! You're messing with us."

"Zoe, I'll say it *again*. That is *not how I talk*."

"Yeah, Zoe. Arcade would say that inquiry, and all that other stuff . . . is DOPE."

"Yeah, Zoe. Inquiry's DOPE."

Zoe chuckled. "Well, you do have inquiry skills. In an annoying sort of way."

"You mean he asks lots of questions? Ha! You got that right."

"But I don't do it to be annoying, you guys! I want to find out things for a reason."

"What reason?"

I pushed my glasses up on my nose. "So I can understand *everything*. So I can understand *everyone*. So I can help."

Zoe looked me straight in the eyes. "Okay, little bro. I believe that to be true about you. But it's still annoying."

The elevator started to ping, and we hit bottom.

The elevator doors do not open this time. Instead, they turn transparent, and I feel like we're in a giant test tube. We're looking out at the darkness, but we're not in the dark, because light is radiating from that golden dome.

Zoe leans back against a wall of the tube. "I know where we are. And I *don't* like it."

I grin. "I know where we are too."

Doug shoves in next to us. "I don't know where we are. Anyone want to clue me in?"

We both say it at the same time. "Mariana Trench."

Doug puts his hand to his throat. "That's deep."

Zoe nods. "The deep-EST. Thanks to Arcade." She smacks me in the shoulder with the back of her hand.

Doug presses both hands to his cheeks. "How long till we get crushed under the pressure?" He looks at me. "There's a lot of pressure at the bottom of the ocean, right?"

Zoe points up. "I think as long as we're under the golden dome, we're protected. So nobody get any crazy ideas about opening those doors." She walks in a little circle in the golden tube. "Sure seems like the loneliest place we've traveled to. Lonelier than the Moon, even."

I gaze out into the dark waters. "Maybe because on the Moon we could see Earth. And that was home. I can't see home here. Can't see anything, actually." I close my eyes tight, and open them again, hoping to see something, anything, swimming out there in the murky water. Nothing. "I'm glad you guys are here or I'd be freaked out."

"Come on, sea creatures. You gotta be down here. Swim on by, we're ready for ya!" Doug presses his hands and nose against the transparent door. Still nothing. Just light rays shining from our golden tube into the pitch blackness.

"I've read about this place. It's called Challenger Deep. There're all kinds of stories about what might live here. From little sea cucumbers, to alien jellyfish, to Megalodons."

"Megalodons? You serious, Arcade?"

"Well, maybe they're stories, and maybe they're truths. More people have been in space than have been down here."

Zoe rubs her arms. "I can see why. It's eerie."

"Nothing but darkness, pressure, and isolation . . . it doesn't feel good, guys." Doug slips an arm around my shoulder and grips hard. "Is your token back yet, Arcade? I'd like to get outta here. I'd go to Everest any day over this."

"Did you know you could drop Everest in here and water would still cover it?"

Zoe gives me the stink-eye. "Thank you, Arcade, for that comforting tidbit of information."

I tap my chest, as if that's going to bring Triple T back from the mold.

What exactly does bring it back?

I sit on the floor of the tube and throw out inquiries. "Zoe, what do all our adventures have in common?"

"In common? Arcade, I don't know! They've all been so different! Scary, random, crazy, emotional, informative—"

I jump up. "That's it!"

"Scary, random, crazy, emotional, or informative?"

"All of those!"

Doug palms the top of my head. "The pressure's getting to him."

I push his hand off. "On every adventure, I've learned something." I point to Zoe. "From the very first adventure, on Bone Crusher, when I said our new life in New York City was like a rodeo . . ."

"And clearly it wasn't." Zoe rolls her eyes.

"Exactly! And every trip since. I learned something."

"Okay, I'll agree with that."

Now Doug palms Zoe's head. "You agree with Arcade? I think the pressure's getting to *you* now."

She pushes his hand off.

"And, check it out, what does the plaque say?" I point to the golden dome. 'Knowledge and belief of truth is the sovereign good of human nature.' I think I'm starting to figure out the truth about myself."

"You're figuring out the truth about yourself?"

"Yeah, Doug, that's what I said."

"What is it, Arcade?" My sister was staring right into my eyes.

"I read a lot of books and ask questions so I can uncover truth. And the main reason I want to know truth is so I can help people. And it's not weird that I'm that way. God made me that way. The truth about me is . . . I'm an *-EST*."

"Oh really?" Zoe crosses her arms. "What kind of –EST are you?"

"I'm God's B–EST. And I need to share with others that they're God's B–EST too."

"Look! A cucumber!" Doug points to something dark floating by in the water.

"That could just be the shadow of your finger, Doug." I laugh.

"Oh. That's too bad. The thought of a cucumber is making me hungry." Doug shoves his hands in his hoodie pockets. "So, what have you learned about the deepest place in the world, Arcade?"

I put an arm around Doug. "That's easy. No one should have to handle darkness and pressure all alone."

Doug sighs. "Oh, man, that's the *truth*."

"So I'm going with you to see the social worker. And I'm going to stay by your side until this whole adoption thing is worked out."

Doug breathed out a sigh. "I think instead of being afraid of heights all this time, I've just been afraid that I'll fall and no one will care enough to catch me."

Zoe came in and gave Doug a hug. "We care, Doug."

Our golden capsule begins to ping again, and I feel a plunk on my chest. Triple T is back from the mold, its mission accomplished, I guess. Light swirls throughout the room as the transparent doors turn gold again and the elevator rises.

There is no coin slot this time. I suppose it's because we never left the elevator, the submarine, the capsule, or whatever this is.

And WHAT IS UP with that mysterious gold dome?

The elevator returned us to our cold New York City street. Doug, Zoe, and I walked silently down the blocks that lead to 88th Street. As usual, there were lots of people walking by us on both sides. Some were alone.

I smiled and waved, and I even stopped to help an elderly woman open her umbrella as some rain began to fall.

"Would you like me to walk you home?"

The lady gave me a shocked look, but then smiled. "Thank you, young man, but I live right around the corner."

I nodded. "Okay. Take care and watch your step. These streets can be slick."

She grinned. "Thank you and bless you."

Zoe pulled up her hood to protect her hair from the mist. And then an umbrella appeared above her head, in the hands of Michael Tolley.

"Zoe, we have to talk." Michael gently took Zoe's hand. "I really like you. I'm so sorry for calling you stubborn."

"Stubborn-EST." Zoe glanced over at me and winked.

"What?"

"You called me the stubborn-EST, Michael."

Michael dropped his chin. "I did. I'm so sorry."

"It's okay. You were right."

"I was?"

Zoe laughed. "Yeah. I'm an -EST. God made me that way for a reason. It's a gift. I just need to learn how to use it to help people."

That made us all laugh. And then it started to pour.

CHAPTER 29
Friday Morning Freak-Out

*K*nock! Knock! Knock!

I rolled over in bed, shoved my glasses on, and checked the clock.

Five a.m.? I hope I'm dreaming . . . again.

A few minutes later, someone shook me. "Arcade, honey, you have visitors downstairs."

Ignore that. You're dreaming.

"Arcade." Mom pulled the blankets off me. "The Tolley brothers are downstairs and they say it can't wait. Please go down there and try to keep the noise down."

"Mom, why didn't you tell them to come back later?"

"Because they said it can't wait."

I sighed and rolled out of bed. "Okay."

My room was cold. So were my feet. "It's Friday. Gotta wear some crazy socks!" I shuffled over to my dresser and searched my sock drawer. "Oh, man, I forgot all about these!" I pulled on a pair of socks that had tropical fish swimming all over them, with a prickly puffer right on the top of both feet. "Perfect for Friday mornings with the Tolleys." I grabbed a blanket and draped it around my shoulders. Loopy had made himself cozy in my warm blankets. "Goofy furball." I headed downstairs.

"Hey, Arcade, glad you're up. We need some help with our Civil War persuasive speeches. We gotta give them today in Harris's class."

"Yeah. Casey's got the north position, and I got the south. And we got good arguments on both sides."

I rubbed my eyes. "Sounds like you're prepared. Why do you need me at five a.m.?"

"Why do we *need* you? Dude, the Civil War was a difficult time in history. People might get riled up. Get mad at us for having an opinion different from theirs."

"It's just an assignment, guys. You're only presenting a side. It doesn't mean it's your actual opinion." I pushed my glasses up higher on my nose. "Plus, since when do *you* care what people think about you?"

"We *always* care."

I scratched my head. "Really?"

"What, you think just because we're tough guys we don't have feelings?"

Yeah. Maybe. I mean, sort of.

Right then, Zoe came down the stairs. Thankfully, she wasn't wearing her reindeer onesie. She was dressed for a run, but it had to be thirty degrees outside.

"Oh, hey, Kevin, Casey." She shot me a funny glance.

"Hi, Zoe." Casey Tolley grinned, revealing his chipped tooth. "You look really nice today."

Zoe gave a smirk. "Well, it's early, but . . . thank you?"

Kevin chimed in. "Michael really likes you."

Zoe turned toward them and put a hand on her hip. "Why are you guys here at the crack of dawn?"

"Tryin' to get help from our favorite bookworm. Not sure what to do about a school assignment. We're caught in the middle of two opinions, and our teacher forced us to choose one."

"And it's a lot harder than choosing what flavor donut to eat in the morning, if you know what I mean."

Zoe nodded and then looked at me. "Well, you can always count on Arcade for an opinion. And if you want the exact opposite viewpoint, just ask me." She smiled, but then . . .

"Arcaaaade . . ."

Kevin Tolley's eyes zoomed in on my chest. "What kind of a goofy nightlight you got there, Arcade?"

OH. NO. THIS CAN'T BE HAPPENING!

I pulled my blanket in front of my chest to try to block the spectrum of light that was shooting out from the Triple T Token. It was no use. This was happening—WITH THE TOLLEYS!

Kevin and Casey stood there, frozen, their eyes following the dazzling light show on the floor, the walls, and the ceiling.

"Guys, stay right there. Zoe, can I talk to you in the kitchen for a minute?' I grabbed her arm and we ran out of the room. The light followed.

"ZOE, I don't know what to do!"

Zoe crossed her arms. "That's ridiculous. You've been doing this for awhile now. You simply grab the token and pull it off the chain."

"Not that! I mean—the TOLLEYS? They can't go on an adventure!"

She held her hands out. "Why not? Amber went. Carlos went. Celeste, Derek, Doug, and Scratchy went. Jacey and Michael went."

"But . . ."

The light shot out past the kitchen and filled the dining room, living room, and entryway.

"But what?"

"But WHAT? They're the TOLLEYS! They'll ruin it! They'll tell people! And maybe they'll even try to take it from me, like the Badgers did!"

Zoe leaned against the wall and stared out at the light. "When we were way down in the Mariana Trench, weren't you telling me that the reason you think you have this dazzling truth detector is so you can learn things in order to *help* people? Was that whole-EST business just a bunch of baloney?"

"Well, no, but—"

"So here you go, Arcade. Two people came at five in the morning for your help. Are you going to deny them because they're . . ." Zoe snapped her fingers as she searched for the word.

I looked down at my puffer fish socks. "Prickly?"

Zoe laughed. "Yes! Prickly."

The light kept getting brighter and brighter. I stepped out from our kitchen area. The beams swirled together and began to form the shape of an elevator, right in front of our door.

"WHAT IS THAT?" Kevin and Casey backed up into me.

"Um, it's a long story that I don't have time to tell you right now, because in just a second a golden coin slot is going to appear and I'm going to have to throw this arcade token in."

"REALLY? COOL! And then what'll happen? Is the place gonna explode?" Casey grabbed on to his brother's shoulder.

"Dude, is this some crazy new virtual gaming system? Because if it is, it's off the hook!"

"No, it's much better than that," Zoe said. "You guys ready for an adventure?"

Casey pointed a thumb my way. "You comin', Arcade?"

The coin slot rose up from the floor, shimmering, glowing, like a fourth of July cone fountain. The flickering lights formed the words GET TRUTH right in midair.

"Yeah, I'm down."

I pulled the token from my chain and reached for the slot. I turned back to look at the Tolleys.

I can't believe I'm doing this!

I dropped the token in.

"Give us some truth about making hard decisions."

I pressed my hands together and pulled them apart.

The elevator and the golden dome shined brighter than ever.

"Are we in some kind of museum?" Kevin pointed to the dome. "What's with all the statues and signs?"

I shrugged. "I haven't figured that out yet. Can you guys read any of the signs?"

Kevin looked up and squinted. "Nah. Too high. Looks like there's a person up at the top, though."

Casey tried to find footing to climb the wall. "Are we gonna shoot out of that hole?"

Zoe chuckled. "We haven't yet. But there's always a first time."

"Are we gonna miss class today? Cause I'm good with that," Kevin said.

"Well, in all my travels, we return right where we left and at the same time."

"All your travels? Where you been, Arcade?" Casey stopped trying to climb and turned around to listen.

"Let's see . . ." I rested my hand on my chin. "Holland, Egypt, Africa, the moon . . ."

"The *moon*?! You're makin' that up." Casey moved in closer. "Sounds like historical fiction, if you ask me."

"Dude, how could I make *this* up?" I raised my palms to the ceiling and turned in a circle.

DING!

CHAPTER 30
The Decision Maker

The doors open up to a dimly lit office. It's not fancy, but there are many pieces of furniture—a couple of couches, chairs, and three desks. The biggest desk sits in the middle of the room. There's a small window in the corner. A tall man stands with his back to us, looking out.

"What should we do, Arcade?" Kevin Tolley steps back into the elevator. "What if he sees us?" Casey is standing next to Kevin, squishing him into a corner.

Are we invisible?

I rub my arms, take a deep breath, and step out.

"Excuse me, sir, we're sorry to bother you."

The man startles and turns. I can hardly believe my eyes.

"Oh, hello, young people." The man looks around the room. "Where did you come from?"

He appears tired and troubled about something. And I've read my history, so I know it's a *lot* of somethings. I decide to just tell him the truth.

"My name is Arcade Livingston, and I'm from New York City."

His mouth turns up in a grin. "A New Yorker, huh?"

"Yes, sir. And I have this golden token that takes my friends and me on adventures in a golden elevator. It teaches us about travel, testing, and, lately, truth. We never know where it's going to land. But today it brought us to your . . . uh . . . office."

He looks around. "I know, it doesn't look like much. But many truths have been revealed to me within these walls."

Zoe walks around the room, smoothing her hand along the surfaces of the desks. "This is unbelievable." She looks up at the man. "We're sorry to have bothered you. You look busy."

He holds up one hand. "It is no bother. What can I do for you?"

"Well," Casey speaks up, "our friend Arcade here is a bookworm, and we—"

"Books?" The man's eyes light up. "I love books too. I always say that my best friend is a person who will give me a book I haven't read."

Man, why don't I have a book with me?

"Yeah," Casey continues, "so since Arcade is smart and all, we asked him to help us make a decision about something. Something really hard. And then this mysterious elevator brought us here."

"You know something about making hard decisions, don't you, sir?" I walk around the room, in awe. "I've read about them."

His eyebrows raise. "You have?" He comes over and touches my sleeve. "Your clothes look very comfortable."

"Oh. These are my pajamas. I'm so sorry. I didn't have time to get dressed."

The man with the dark features surveys our group carefully. "It's interesting timing that all of you should show up. It confirms a big decision I am about to make. I've been thinking, praying, and obtaining counsel. Would you like to watch me sign a proclamation?"

He walks over to a hat rack, pulls out a tall top hat, and places it on his head. Kevin goes ballistic.

"It's YOU! I knew you looked familiar!"

"And I know what you're about to do!" Casey hits himself in the forehead. "I've been studying all about it! This ROCKS, man!"

"Rocks?" The man tilts his head.

"He means," Zoe says, "that this is a wonderful moment in history."

He nods. "I never in my life have felt more certain that I was doing right, than I do signing this paper. But not everyone will agree. Our struggles will not end here."

"Then how can you do it?" Casey comes in closer. "How can you make the decision when you know people will disagree with you?"

Abraham Lincoln sits down at his desk, picks up a pen, and dips it in ink. "He has shown you, O mortal, what is good. And what does the Lord require of you? To act justly and to love mercy and to walk humbly with your God."

I finger my gold chain.

I love truth.

And then Zoe, Kevin, Casey, and I stand around our

sixteenth president's desk and watch
him sign the Emancipation
Proclamation!

"This is DOPE!"

Mr. Lincoln tilts
his head. "Dope?"

Zoe laughs. "He
means, this is fantastic."

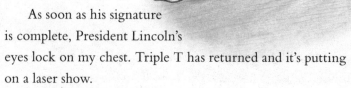

As soon as his signature
is complete, President Lincoln's
eyes lock on my chest. Triple T has returned and it's putting
on a laser show.

He stands and removes his hat. "That is a spectacular
token, Arcade. I'm glad it chose to bring you here to visit
me today." He hangs his head. "I am sorry I was not much
help to you children. Perhaps next time?"

We make our way to the elevator doors that have
appeared back in the office.

"Mr. President, what you did today helped us greatly. I
guarantee it." Zoe smiles and joins me near the coin slot that
has risen from the floor and is pulsating light toward the
token.

"I wish we could stay longer and ask you a ton of
questions." I pull the token from the chain and drop it into
the slot. I make the open-door motion with my hands, and
the antique gold doors open.

"You are welcome back any time." President Lincoln
holds his pen out to me. "Would you like to take this
with you?"

I'm sure my eyes light up as bright as Elena's.

"YES! But . . . won't they want to put this in a museum one day?"

"An old pen? I can't imagine. But if they do, I'll just have to give them another one." Abraham Lincoln laughs and shakes my hand before giving me the pen.

"Thank you, sir. And next time, I'll bring you a book about one of the great-EST presidents in United States history."

He raises an eyebrow. "Really? I look forward to reading all about him."

On the ride back, the Tolleys can't stop talking about Abraham Lincoln and how excited they are to give their speeches in class.

"Arcade, you're the best! Thanks for the help, man." Kevin smiles, and comes over to shake my hand.

The elevator dings and the golden doors slide open.

Casey pats me on the chest. "And don't you worry, Arcade. Your secret is safe with us."

H OW could you go see *Abraham Lincoln* without me?"
Doug munched a bowl of cereal as we all gathered our
supplies for school.

"I'm sorry. You were sleeping, and you know how the
token has a mind of its own. I had no idea we were going
anywhere."

Doug shoveled a huge spoonful in his mouth and took a
minute to swallow. "Yeah, I get it. I probably would have set
the Tolleys off somehow. But I wonder if President Lincoln
would have some good advice for me about my appointment
today with the social worker."

"I'm SURE he would. Hey—that reminds me of
something."

"What?" Doug gulped his last bite of cereal.

"He gave me a souvenir."

"He gave you a souvenir? That's cool! What did he
give you?"

"I'll show you later."

"Aw, man!"

Mom and Dad picked us up after school. It's a rare thing since everything is so close in the city that we can walk or take the subway. But today, Doug's appointment was downtown, and we couldn't be late.

Doug's social worker greeted us and then invited us into her office. "Would you like some coffee or hot chocolate and a cookie?"

"Hot chocolate, please." I turned to Doug. "You want something?"

Doug stood, stiff in the doorway. "No, thank you, ma'am." He shuffled to the chair in the corner and sat down.

Mom and Dad took a seat on the chairs in front of the desk. I stood over by Doug. The social worker brought in three hot chocolates and cookies on a platter, handed them to us, and then sat down behind her desk. She opened a large file folder.

"Doug, first I'd like to say how sorry I am about your grandmother. I know this is a hard bit of news to accept. I was over at her facility today, and she was having a good day. I'm hoping they'll find some medication that will make this whole process easier for her."

Doug still sat stiffly. "Thank you, ma'am."

"Your aunt is ready to move you in to her house today. She's informed the school, has your room ready, and said she'll book your flight out as soon as you say the word. She really wants to be your guardian."

Doug's shoulders drooped. "That's very nice of her."

Come on, Doug, fight!

"But you can choose other guardians."

Doug's head popped up. "What did you say?"

"You can choose *other* guardians. For example, you could choose the two people who are sitting across from my desk right now."

"But I thought I *had* to go to Florida, since Gram doesn't know who I am anymore."

The social worker smiled. "Well, she knew who you were today. She showed me a bunch of pictures and told me some really funny stories about you."

"She did?"

"Yes. The doctor was there too. He was able to assess her and attest to the fact that she knew what she was doing when she signed this paper."

Doug stood up and walked over to the desk. "What paper?"

"The one that gives up her guardianship rights." The social worker held the paper out for Doug to see. "I know this is hard, Doug. She cried when she did it. But she wants the best for you, and she understands that she may not get better. And now you can permanently go to your aunt's, or . . ."

"Or what?"

"You can be officially adopted . . . by these people."

I expected Doug to jump up and down and give us all high fives. But he just turned and looked down at the floor.

"You have all been so kind to me. And I would love to be adopted by you. But I don't want you to feel pressure. I know I'm a handful, and I eat a lot, and I don't have a job, and you didn't expect to add another kid to your family when you moved to New York City, that's for sure. And just wait till the bills for culinary school kick in—"

"Doug, stop." Mom stood up, walked over, and put her hand on his shoulder.

"Yeah, Doug," I said. "Why are you trying to talk us out of it?"

"You don't have any more bedrooms. That means you're stuck with me on the top bunk. And Zoe—she sure doesn't need another annoying brother."

"Hey, are you calling me *annoying*?"

"Am I calling you annoying?"

"That's what I said, Doug."

"Well, I just want to make sure you guys know what you're doing. Once you adopt me, I'm there for good, making pasta in your kitchen. Forever."

Dad stood. "I love pasta. Where do I sign?"

The social worker looked at Doug. "Doug, it's your decision. What do you choose to do?"

Doug's eyes lit up. "Are you kiddin'? I want to be a Livingston!"

Mom hugged Doug. So did Dad. So did I.

"Where do we sign?" Dad asked, and the social worker pulled out a few papers. "We'll have to wait for an official date for the courthouse ceremony, but as long as none of you change your mind, you can consider this final."

"Where do *I* sign?" Doug asked as he took a bite of *my* cookie.

"Oh, you don't have to sign, since you're a minor."

"But I really want to!"

The social worker smiled. "Okay. Why don't you sign . . ." She looked for a white space on the official form. "Here."

"Hold up!" I grabbed my backpack and opened the front pocket. "I've got just the pen for this!" I reached down and pulled out the historic gift from President Lincoln. It still had a bit of ink left in the end. "Here." I handed it to Doug. "A souvenir to remember this special moment."

"A souvenir?"

"Yes. Do the right thing with it."

Doug took the pen up to the desk. The social worker pointed out the white space for his signature. "I'm never felt so right about a decision in my life." Doug grinned, and then he signed his official adoption papers with Abraham Lincoln's Emancipation Proclamation pen!

That's dope!

CHAPTER 32

Arcade
Con

The next two weeks were full of trips to see Doug's grandma, who had been feeling better, to the social worker to turn in a bit more paperwork, and to the bakery to get ideas for Doug's official adoption cake, which he insisted he was going to make.

And each day that ticked by brought us closer to February twenty-third.

"Hey, Arcade." Zoe snuck into my room one Sunday night after Doug was asleep. "Check this out." She pulled up a social media account that was set up for a local event— Arcade Con.

She scrolled through the posts. "These arcade conventions are put on by, get this, the Double T Gaming Company! Says here they supply equipment for the most popular arcades in the country."

"Double T?"

She nodded. "I know. And I have to show you this one picture in their gallery." She scrolled some more. "Their catalog lists different game machines available for purchase.

Does this claw machine look familiar?" She showed me
one that looked just like the one Dad played at Arcade
Adventures when he won the token. "They also have rides,
video games, and what I really want you to see is . . ." She
scrolled way down. "Oh, where did it go? Ah! Here it is.
Try not to let your jaw hit the floor."

She held the phone out. The picture was an ad offering
entire sets of equipment, including miniature golf courses!
The one she showed me was called the Journey Course,
complete with waterfall, bridge, village house, and a
windmill.

"What?!?"

"Exactly! And check *this* out. It says here that 'each
feature comes with a golden plaque with the words *Humility*,
Generosity, *Forgiveness*, and *Restoration*'! And you can have
your business's name engraved on the plaques."

"Zoe! This is where the Badger brothers purchased their
windmill course!"

"Yep. And that explains why Arcade Adventures was
engraved on all those plaques. They bought the course
before they changed the name from Arcade Adventures to
Forest Games and Golf."

She pointed to another ad. "They must have purchased
these too. Double T golden game tokens! Available with
business name engraved on the back. Five thousand tokens
per package."

"But *Double T*? My token has three Ts."

Zoe pushed me over in my bed. "Arcade! Your token
didn't come from this company. It came from one-hundred

percent pure gold that was cast in the mold shaped by Theo Timon Theros."

"I know that, Zoe." I stared at the tokens on the social media site. They were similar to mine, but not real gold. The Ts in the front were connected, but there were only two.

"Arcade, don't you get it?"

I scratched my head. "No."

"Ruah."

"Ruah?"

"Yes! Ruah told Theo she would find the one who could live out his wish. She must have been searching, and when she saw this, Arcade Adventures, just like on Theo's mold, and Double T? That's close enough! And knowing that a kid might end up with the token—"

"Wait. Do you think she planted it somehow? Either at Arcade Adventures or in the Badger brothers' token order, hoping a kid would win it at one of the games?"

"I think that's exactly what she did. But the Badgers found it first."

Doug's head popped down from his bunk. "Hey! Can't a brother get some sleep around here?"

Zoe jumped. "Doug! Don't scare us like that!"

"Are you guys gonna fill me in on what's goin' on?"

"Yeah." I pulled on Doug's arm. "Get down here. We gotta find out everything we can about Arcade Con."

Doug dropped down from his bunk and sat cross-legged on my bed. "Why?"

Zoe smirked. "So we can keep an eye on the Badgers, and find out if this Kenwood thing is a setup."

"Yeah," I punched my pillow. "Let's spy on *them* for a change."

Doug thrust out a fist. "GAME ON."

Saturday afternoon—two days before Arcade Con—Zoe, Doug, and I sat outside on our cold brownstone steps and came up with our plan.

"It says here Arcade Con starts Monday at noon and ends Wednesday at noon." Zoe held her phone up so we could view the website. "No school on Monday. Could we go then?"

Doug scrolled through his phone calendar. "That's when we're all supposed to spend the afternoon with Gram."

"That's important." I scrolled through the Arcade Con website. "We can go Tuesday. I think we can assume the Badgers will be there." I pressed the button to register as a guest for the expo. "Oh, no! The tickets are fifty dollars *a person* to get into the expo area. We can't afford that!"

Zoe patted the small pocket of her backpack. "Oh, yes we can. I'm the saver of the family, remember?"

"Zoe, you would do that for me?"

"Of course! But you'll be paying me back."

"Pay you back? I *never* have that kind of cash."

"Did I say you had to pay me in *cash*? Chores will do, and you can start by paying me tonight. Mom and Doug are making spaghetti, and that means a lot of pots and pans to wash."

Doug patted me on the shoulder. "I'll try not to make too big a mess."

That night, we purchased our Arcade Con expo passes online. We printed them out and stuffed them in our notebooks.

"Are you ready?" Doug laughed.

"Oh, yeah." I pumped my fist in the air. "We're doin' this!"

I saw Elena Salvador Castro many times on Tuesday, February twenty-second. She met me after every class, and we said the same thing to each other every time.

"Hey, Livingston."

"Hi, Elena. Did I tell you how great these glasses are?"

She smiled. "Yes. I'm glad they're working well. Have you decided to run for student body president yet? The paperwork is due Friday."

"Really?" I adjusted my glasses. "I don't know if I SEE myself doing that just yet." I put one hand over my left eye and began to yell out letters. "A . . . R . . . C . . . A . . . D . . . E . . . F . . . O . . . R . . ."

"Go on," she said.

"I'm sorry. Can't read the last line."

She shook her head. "You're a funny boy, Livingston." Then she took off with her permanent hall pass to go bug someone else.

The day crept on. The closer it got to dismissal, the

higher my blood pressure rose. Right before Doug took off to his last period history class, I looked him in the eye.

"We gotta get out fast today. Meet me out front as soon as you can, and we'll run to the subway to meet Zoe. We need to catch the earliest train down to the convention center."

"Gotcha!" Doug whispered, and he took off down the hall to his classroom.

Of course, in PE, we were playing *another* co-ed volleyball tournament. But this time, the boys and girls were mixed.

Elena was on my team.

"Hey, Livingston! Let's get 'em! With my hands and your face, we can rule the court."

We did make a good team. We smoked everyone. It was like I could see the ball clearer than ever before with my magical glasses from Castro Optometry.

After the tournament, Elena came up and gave me a high five. "You play like a student body president. Papers are due Friday."

"I'll think about it on Friday."

I was a sweaty mess by the time I changed out of my gym clothes, ran to meet Doug, and then rushed through the park and across the street to meet Zoe at the subway station.

"Tell me you brought your metro cards." Zoe held up her card as we followed her down the steps to the turnstile.

"I got mine!" Doug swiped his through the card reader.

I held mine up. "I'm a pro at this now."

As we stood in the crowded car that would take us down near Bryant Park, Zoe leaned over and whispered in my ear. "We stay together for this, Arcade. Just like always. I don't care who we see or what they do, or even what Triple T does. I don't trust the Badgers for one second."

The expo room in the convention center was slammed with people. The man at the entrance gave us a funny look.

"Our family is very interested in arcades." I grinned. The man nodded and scanned our tickets.

Zoe rolled her eyes.

"What? I told the truth. You guys are really interested in me, right?"

The place was set up like a huge arcade resort; games were everywhere, chiming, ringing, and pinging. Sales representatives stood next to the games ready to demo, explain terms, and sign contracts. A few inflatable rooms were set up, and I wondered what kind of laser tag or mystery obstacles lurked inside.

"This would be a cool job," Doug said. "I can see why the Badgers were interested in—"

Zoe grabbed my elbow. "Badger at three o'clock!" She pulled me behind a tall game console.

Doug ducked in with us. "And there's another one at three-thirty."

I peeked around the game.

They wore the same outfit—just like the Tolleys do most of the time. Dark blue jeans, black, long-sleeved

T-shirts, and dark green sleeveless puff vests that had the Forest Games and Golf logo on the left breast pocket. They walked from one vendor to another, chatting, laughing, and looking like brothers WHO GET ALONG.

"We gotta get where we can hear what they're saying." I poked my head out from behind the game to find a safe spy route.

Zoe shook an index finger at me. "Careful! We CAN'T let them see us."

"It would be nice to be token invisible right now," Doug said.

We followed the Badgers, sneaking behind displays, banners, and tall games. We stopped and listened when they came to a table where they seemed to know a guy.

"Lenwood and Kenwood Badger! How long has it been?" The guy stuck out a hand and high-fived both brothers. "How are things at Arcade Adventures? Wait, you changed the name, right? I remember when I sold you that windmill course. You were my first big sale. Took the family to Hawaii with the commission money."

One of the brothers smiled. "Never better, Andrew. Never better. In fact, business is so good, we're expanding. The land came up for sale next to us, so we're thinking of putting in another course."

Andrew pulled a brochure out of his briefcase. "That's great news! Wait till you see our newest models. It's a whole new world out there in the land of mini-golf."

"Well, let's see what you got!" The other brother moved in, and they took forever to look over everything.

"Zoe. I gotta move."

Zoe grabbed me. "You'll stay right here."

"Hey, guys, look!" Doug's mouth hung open as he pointed to a woman standing next to a large video game console. She was wearing a white sweat suit and a ballcap.

"Ruah." I said it quietly, stepping out from behind the banner so she could see me. She turned her head, and the Triple T logo on her hat began to shoot out beams toward my chest.

"No, no, no, no, no, NO! This can't happen right now!" I covered my token, which hung under my thick sweatshirt. I looked down at my hand. Thankfully, it wasn't glowing.

But the whole place was. And the volume of every game console got louder, and dazzling lights flashed all over the walls—just like the time when my mom and dad pulled the token out of the claw machine at Arcade Adventures.

The crowd went wild with clapping.

Is this a demo? Maybe an intro to the grand finale of the expo?

I grabbed Zoe's arm and pulled her out from behind the banner toward the exit. Doug followed close behind. I turned to wave to Ruah, but instead of seeing her, I locked eyes with a Badger! He frowned, clicked his pen a couple times, and slammed it down on the table. Then he came after us!

"LET'S JET!"

We ran past the ticket scanner guy, down the stairs, out of the building, onto the sidewalk, and past one, two, three subway stations before we finally had to stop and rest.

I bent over and gasped for breath. "You think they followed us?"

Zoe heaved in air. "They might have tried. But we were flying. I think we lost them."

"Either way, I don't want to get stuck in a subway car with them." I kept a close eye, left and right, for green puff vests.

"Me either." Zoe pointed north, toward Central Park. "I think we should zig-zag our way through the crowds."

Doug grabbed his throat. "All the way home?"

Zoe nodded. "Yeah. All the way home."

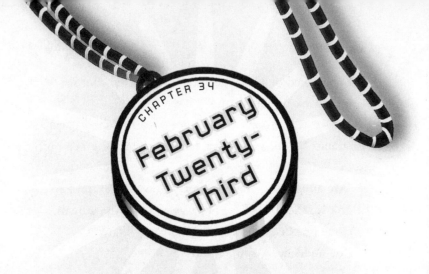

CHAPTER 34

February Twenty-Third

nd as your Student Body President, I promise to build our school the biggest library in the world . . ."

"You can't do that, Arcade. You have a blocked library card."

I woke up in a pool of sweat.

"WHAT?!?!?"

Doug jumped down from his bunk. "WHAT?!?!?"

"That's what I said."

"I KNOW. You woke me up. AGAIN!" He grabbed his belly and looked at the clock. "It's four a.m. And now I'm hungry."

I jumped out of bed. "Will you make me some of your famous waffles? I need a hearty breakfast if I'm going to have a showdown with the Badgers today."

"You got it, bro!"

"And I have a plan, so I need to get started."

I threw on clothes before going downstairs. By that time, Doug was already mixing waffle batter and had bacon frying in a pan.

"That's gonna wake people up. But it smells good!"

Doug whipped the batter with a whisk. "Only the best for showdown day." He tipped his head toward the dining room table. "Looks like Dad left you a note."

"He must have written this a little bit ago."

My mouth dropped open when I read it.

> *Get the truth and never sell it; also get*
> *wisdom, discipline, and good judgment.*
> —— PROVERBS 23:23 NLT ——

"That's a good one!" Doug poured batter onto the hot waffle iron. "Did he write anything else?"

"Yeah." I took a breath before reading.

> *Arcade, I'm so proud of the young man*
> *you are becoming. Remember to keep the*
> *important things close.*
> —Dad

I slapped the note with the back of my hand. "This is crazy. CRAZY. How does Dad know? Every time I get in a golden elevator, it says GET TRUTH. And now Dad gives me this note."

Doug wiped his hands on his pajama pants and came

over to look at the note. "Parents are hard to figure out. But whatever you do, I'd keep the important things close." He patted me on the shoulder.

I looked up at Doug. "Whatever happens this afternoon, you stay right beside me, okay?"

"You got it." Doug smiled. "Thanks, Arcade."

The rest of that early morning we munched on waffles and bacon, and we put together a list of the people who had been through the golden elevator doors with me over the last ten months. "Let's see, there was Amber Lin."

"The dog surgeon?"

I grinned. "Yeah. That was nuts. I wonder how our K-9, Samson, is doing. Oh, and Scratchy."

Doug popped bacon in his mouth. "Pit crew man and pilot!"

"Well, hardly. That couldn't have been a real plane. And

Carlos. I wish you had been there to see him walking up in the crown of the Statue of Liberty."

"That would have been amazing. Instead, I was hanging out with plastic flamingos in Florida. Glad I'm not going back there."

I scrolled through the names on my phone and selected them for a group text. "Man, I wish Celeste and Derek lived here."

Doug punched my arm. "Don't forget about Jacey."

"Okay, fine. Jacey too." I gave him the slightest grin. When I got to the Ts, I hesitated. "All three Tolleys know about the token now! That blows my mind. How did that happen, Doug?"

Doug wiped butter from the corner of his mouth. "Well, it is a *Triple T* Token. Maybe it stands for the three Tolleys."

"Haha, good one." I added all three Tolleys to the text.

"Don't forget to add *me*." Zoe had snuck up behind me and flicked the back of my head. I jumped about a mile. "I've been on every adventure since you got that crazy token."

I showed my list to Zoe. "Can you remember anyone else?"

She sat down next to me and thought for a moment. "Well, there was that time when the Badgers hitched a ride to San Francisco. But I wouldn't add them to this text. What do you plan to write on this text anyway, Arcade?"

I typed away as Doug and Zoe watched over my shoulder.

Hey friends. Going on an Arcade adventure today. Wanna come? Meet me at the Bow Bridge in Central Park at 4:00 p.m. sharp. Keep on the down low.

Zoe pressed her hands on the table. "Hang on, Arcade. You're going to get them *all* together, *with the Badgers*? What if the token doesn't do anything? This is what you call a plan?"

I nodded. "Yeah. You like it?"

"NO! There's a whole lot of madness that could happen right there. And really, Arcade? The Tolleys?"

"Well, you don't have a problem with inviting Michael, do you? My plan is to show the Badger brothers all the people who've been helped by the token. That's the real value of it."

"Ha, too bad we can't have Flames the flamingo with us too." Doug went over to the waffle iron to scoop in another glob of batter.

"Plus, we'll be in the middle of Central Park, with tons of other people. What could go wrong?" I raised my shaking index finger and pushed send on the text message.

Zoe closed her eyes. "Well, there's no going back now!" She grabbed me by the shoulders. "Just promise you'll stay close to me."

I smiled. "I will."

That school day was full of awkwardness. Especially in Dooley's homeroom. Almost everyone on the group text was in that class, and they kept giving me winks and thumbs up.

"MR. LIVINGSTON, HAVE YOU DONE SOMETHING NOTABLE THAT YOU'D LIKE TO SHARE WITH THE CLASS?"

"Excuse me, Mr. Dooley?"

He crossed his arms and jumped up to sit on his desk. "THERE ARE CONGRATULATORY GESTURES FLYING YOUR WAY. CARE TO SHARE?"

Aw, man. Wish I had Elena's cookies this time.

"Um, well . . ."

Kevin Tolley came to my rescue. "Arcade's gonna run for student body president." He began to clap.

The whole class broke out in applause.

Mr. Dooley smiled. "WELL, ARCADE, IT LOOKS LIKE YOU HAVE SOME LOYAL SUPPORTERS. I'D SAY YOU HAVE A GOOD SHOT OF WINNING IF YOU STAY TRUE TO YOURSELF."

I cleared my throat. "Thank you, sir. I will do my best."

What am I saying? I'm not running for student body president!

And of course, the news from class got to Elena Salvador Castro, who hunted me down at lunch with that packet of papers.

"You think these are going to fill themselves out? The deadline's Friday, you know." She tried to put them in my hand, but was interrupted by Amber Lin.

"Arcade, can I talk to you for a minute?" She was holding her phone.

"Sorry, gotta go, Elena."

Elena laughed. "How convenient. Just remember, I know where to find you, Livingston. All the kids want you to run. I want you to run. So . . . just run. Okay?" She turned to join the rest of the lunch crowd.

"Hey, Arcade, I was just reading your exciting text! Are you bringing Loopy? Should I bring Snickers?"

Snickers is Amber's very well-behaved chocolate lab.

"Oh, Amber, I don't know about Loopy. You know how bad he is on a leash. I'm gonna leave him at home this time. But you can bring Snickers."

"It's okay. I'll leave her at home. I'll see you at four."

I lifted my eyebrows. "So, you're coming?"

"I wouldn't miss it! Thanks so much for inviting me." Amber gathered her books tighter and walked away.

I put my hand over my Triple T Token.

"I'm gonna trust you have something good planned."

My lunch didn't mix well with all the adrenaline pumping through my body during PE. I had to sit out.

"Stomach cramps?" Mr. Lozano came over. "You're not afraid of volleyballs now, are you?"

"No, sir. Just not feeling my best."

He looked at his watch. "The bell's gonna ring in ten minutes, so go to the locker room and get changed. Take your time. Drink some water. You'll be feeling super by the time you get home."

I stood up, grabbing my stomach. "Thanks."

And where exactly will I travel before I make it home?

The dismissal bell rang at three fifteen.

Forty-five minutes to showdown.

Doug met me out in front of the school. We headed over to the corner and crossed the street which led into Central Park.

"Let's take the Ramble trail." I picked up the pace. "I want to be on the north side of the bridge."

"The north? Why?"

"It's symbolic. I want all our friends to stand behind me, with my home and school located behind them." I checked the time on my phone. "We gotta run, Doug. Just in case anyone shows up early."

We passed by the site of the secret Ramble cave, where we had chased Flames into the golden elevator on his way back to the Beijing Zoo.

We curved around the path by the lake and ran by the snack shop where Carlos and Scratchy met us to look for Loopy when he was lost.

We rounded the last curve, and there it was. The famous Bow Bridge. I checked my phone. Three-forty.

"Arcade!" I turned to see Zoe, running and waving, with Michael Tolley by her side.

Okay, at least there are four of us now. If Amber shows, we'll have five.

"Arcade Livingston."

It was a man's voice . . . right behind me! I turned around. Two Badgers were standing there.

"You're early." I could feel Zoe, Doug, and Michael crowd in close behind me.

"It's good business," one of them said. "On time is late."

"That's what my dad says."

"Your dad is a smart man."

"I invited some friends." I looked around, to see if any more had shown up yet. Nope.

One of the brothers chuckled. "That's fine. We're not asking for trouble. Just the token."

We're?

"It was ours to begin with," the other one said.

Oh, no! This IS a setup!

"I don't understand." My eyes shot from one Badger to the next. I touched the token. "Ruah gave this to me. She said I was the one to have it. I didn't understand why at first, but now I know I'm supposed to use it to help people. It's what I was made to do." Just then, Amber, Scratchy, and Carlos joined us on the bridge.

"What's going on, Arcade? Everything okay?" Scratchy stood there, balancing on his electric scooter.

"Wait for *us*, bro!" The Tolley brothers came running up behind. He looked at the Badgers and pointed at one of them. "Hey, it's you! I met you the other day on Arcade's front steps. Or was it . . . you?"

The Badger on the left turned to the other one. "What's he talking about, Kenwood?"

Kenwood Badger, the brother on the right, stepped forward, into the middle of our group! He turned around to face his brother. "I went to Arcade's house to leave him a note. I wanted us all to meet to discuss the token. This has gone too far, Lenwood. The kid is right. He's the one who should have it. All it did was tear us apart."

Lenwood Badger shoved his hands in his pockets. "No. It was your terrible business sense and lack of drive that tore us apart!"

"I was grieving over the loss of my wife! Don't you have any compassion at all? Arcade fixed our golf course! Can't you see he's got the heart of gold to match the token?"

Lenwood paced back and forth, huffing and puffing across the width of the bridge. He stopped in front of me and pulled a huge wad of cash from his back pocket. "Okay, kid. What's your price? Everyone has a price."

"Seriously, Lenwood? You're going to try to buy it from him? With what money?"

"Oh, I have plenty. While *you* were slacking, *I* was saving." He took a

checkbook out of his back pocket and looked me square in the eyes. "How much? A thousand? Ten thousand? Fifty thousand? How about one hundred thousand?"

Kenwood stepped toward Lenwood. "One hundred thousand? Mind telling me where you got that kind of money?"

"Oh, please. You know where I got it. Arcade Adventures was booming, and I couldn't trust *you* to handle it, so *I* handled it. I put the money in a special account so you couldn't mismanage it."

"You mean you *stole* it? No wonder we didn't have funds to fix the windmill. You were hiding our profits!"

"No. I kept the profits for *this* moment, Kenwood, so we could buy the token back! And once we have it, we'll be successful again." He looked at me. "Do we have a deal?"

I stepped back and grabbed the token. "It's not for sale, sir."

"Aw, come on, kid. Don't try to be some kind of noble superhero."

"I'm sorry, Mr. Badger. I've got the truth now, and I'll *never* sell it."

Lenwood lurched forward to grab me, but Kenwood put both arms out to shield me.

"It stops here, brother. Leave Arcade alone."

"Yeah, leave him alone!" Michael Tolley pushed forward and stood next to Kenwood Badger with his arms out too.

"Yeah, who do YOU think you are? Arcade's a good guy!" Both Kevin and Casey Tolley stepped forward and did the same. Carlos in his wheelchair and Scratchy with his scooter rolled up on both ends of the protective people wall. And Zoe and Amber linked their arms with mine.

Lenwood Badger pushed his brother. "You've always been the weak one. I don't know why I ever went into business with you. So here's what I'm going to do. Since the kid won't take the money, I'm going to use it to start my own business, and I'm going to TAKE YOU DOWN! You'll regret this day forever, brother!" Then he turned and walked back over the bridge, out of sight.

Kenwood Badger's shoulders drooped as he watched his brother walk away. "I had high hopes he would see things more clearly."

"Maybe he needs a little trip to Castro Optometry."

"What?"

I put my hand on his shoulder. "I'm sorry about your business and about your money, Mr. Badger."

Kenwood shook his head. "There's more to life than money. I pray someday Lenwood realizes that." He reached out his hand to shake mine. "I've learned a lot from you, Arcade Livingston. You gave me and my brother a wonderful gift when we didn't deserve it. Only someone with a pure heart would do that. I'm sure more people will be blessed by your generous spirit. Never stop learning and growing. And," he said with a wink, "happy travels."

CHAPTER 38

The Golden Dome

As soon as Kenwood said "happy travels," Triple T came to life! The glow from the dazzling lights lit up the Bow Bridge and the faces of the new friends I had made since moving to New York City eleven months ago.

"Are you guys ready to go somewhere awesome?"

"Yeah!" they all cheered. Kevin and Casey Tolley cheered the loudest.

Two light beams shot out from the token and formed the outline of elevator doors in the middle of the Bow Bridge. The lights solidified into antique gold doors that sparkled as the setting sun hit them. A coin slot rose from the ground, and we watched as a golden sign fell from the sky that said GET TRUTH.

Zoe grabbed my arm tight. "Where are you going to take *all* these people, Arcade?"

I stepped forward, pulled the token from my chain, and dropped it into the slot. "Someplace where they can discover the truth about themselves." I made the open-door motion with my hands. The doors opened to a huge room this time.

I stepped in and tilted my head back to look at the ceiling. "And I want to find out what this gold dome is all about, once and for all."

"Let's goooooo!" Doug shouted, and he ushered our large group in. Carlos, Scratchy, Amber, Zoe, Kevin and Casey Tolley, Michael Tolley, and . . . oh, no . . . wait a minute . . .

"LIVINGSTON! Hey! You can *run* but you can't hide! Are you going to fill out these papers or . . . WHAT IS THIS??!!??"

Elena Salvador Castro.

She slowed, her mouth hanging open as her eyes followed the dazzling lights all over the bridge and in the elevator.

I sighed. "Did you bring a pen?"

Elena stared for a few more moments, but then snapped out of it. "Oh. A pen. Of course." She dug into her backpack and produced a golden pen. "Will this do?" She carefully stepped into the elevator to hand it to me, and her eyes widened.

"Well. It's not as nice as Abraham Lincoln's, but it'll have to do. You may want to hang on—this thing can get pretty bumpy."

She pressed her back against the elevator wall and stared up at the gold dome. "Where are we going?"

I signed the papers, handed them back to her, and shrugged. "Wherever this dazzling truth detector wants to take us. Oh," I shook the pen at her, "but you have to promise me one thing."

She rolled her eyes. "What is it, Livingston?"

"No matter how *fun*, how *incredible*, how *breathtaking* an experience we have together today, you HAVE to promise me that you WON'T want to be my girlfriend."

Everyone in the elevator laughed. Elena grabbed her stomach and doubled over. "Hahahahahahahahaha!" Then she reached over to give me a high five. "Now *that's* a good one. I'm glad you set me straight. I promise!"

Kenwood Badger stood just outside the elevator door, peering in.

"You wanna come, Mr. Badger?"

He put a hand to his heart. "You'd let me come, after everything that's happened?"

I pointed to the golden sign. "Do you want to GET TRUTH?"

Kenwood nodded. "More than anything else."

"Then hop in."

"Yo, Arcade! I was hoping all this blinding light meant you were coming to get us!"

No one was more surprised than me to see the elevator doors open right on top of Aunt Weeda's couch in Virginia, with Derek, Celeste, and Jacey Green waiting to join the party.

"Check it out! I just bought this gold visor." Derek pulled his visor off his head, flipped it upside down, and plopped it back on. "Where we goin', Arcade?"

Jacey stepped in next to me. "New York City?"

"I'm ready for anything." Celeste crowded in next to Doug. "Hey, Dougie."

Doug blushed.

"Who we got in here?" Derek turned around and waved at the confused bunch of travelers I'd picked up on my life's journey over the last eleven months.

I smiled. "A bunch of –ESTS."

Butterflies flew around my insides as the golden elevator glided up, down, and sideways. Thankfully, no spinning.

But there was a lot of buzz in the elevator.

"Where are we going?"

"What is this dome?"

"What do all those plaques say?"

"Is that a person way up there?"

The questions flew out, one by one.

And for once, I was at peace not knowing the answers.

The elevator came to an abrupt halt. The doors slid open to reveal a young man holding a clipboard in what looked like a university building.

"Aahir?"

Aahir looked up from his clipboard and his jaw dropped.

"Arcade? I pressed the button to go to the library. What is happening?"

"I wanted to find you, but Zoe said it would be impossible."

Aahir smiled. "Well, look at you. Making the impossible happen."

"Would you like to come with us? If you need to GET TRUTH, this is the right elevator."

Aahir examined the inside of the elevator. He pushed his glasses up on the bridge of his nose. "I suppose that is what I'm looking for. Is there room?"

"Everybody squeeze!" We all pushed back a little, and Aahir stepped in. "This will be cooler than a flying ostrich. You'll see."

The golden elevator rocked a little, then tipped left and right, but we were packed in so tight, we barely moved. The ride finally smoothed, the elevator dropped slightly, and landed with a gentle thump.

I took a deep breath and blew it out.

DING!

Tears fall from my eyes when the doors open and I see what is in front of me.

Books. Tons of them! Ton *and tons* AND TONS of

them—on shelves, under gold arches, in a gold-toned room—with wooden reading desks and reading lamps . . .

I step out of the elevator and look up.

And a golden dome, just like the one in the elevator!

A young, blonde, college-aged woman approaches our group with a large envelope. "Oh, good, you're here! Ruah said you were on your way."

"Ruah?"

"Yes. She's in charge of our special access passes."

Zoe comes up next to me. "Special access?"

The girl opens the envelope. "Yes. Usually you have to be sixteen to get in here. But we managed to get reader passes for all of you. You must be Arcade Livingston," she says with a smile. She reaches into the envelope and hands me my pass. "Welcome to the Library of Congress—the largest library in the world."

CHAPTER 37

TRUTH

The woman gives special reader passes to all my friends.
I have a hard time swallowing the lump in my throat.

"The Library of Congress," Michael Tolley says, shaking his head in amazement. "I've always wanted to visit. This is magnificent!"

"Ruah said you all had specific research to do. She calls you the Triple T Team."

"Triple T Team? I like that."

"I'd suggest you start with one of our research librarians. They can help you find books on any topic. If you can think of it, we most likely have it." She looks directly at me. "And if you have a specific question about a place, a person, or an item, we can help you find that too."

Doug reaches for his reader pass. "You got cookbooks? Or books on culinary techniques?"

She smiles. "Over five thousand."

Doug's eyes almost pop out of his head.

"How about engineering?" Derek takes off his visor so he can look up at the dome.

"A whole collection. You'll head in that direction for those."

"Where are your travel books? I want to find out about every place I've never been." Jacey beams as she takes off in the direction the woman points out.

Aahir looks at me. "Well, I was on my way to the library to do research for a microbiology project. This is outstanding, Arcade! I will share with you what I find!" He takes off under one of the golden arches.

"I want to be President of the United States someday," Celeste says. "Where do I start?"

The woman gets particularly excited about that. "Political science. Right this way. I'm a political science major!"

All my friends, including Kenwood Badger, take off in the area of their interests. Each one a different direction, each one with a smile on their face. Zoe stays right next to me.

"What, you're not going to check out France or cockatoo management, or books on how to argue? I'm sure they have them here."

"No. I want to see where *you* go. What will Arcade Livingston choose to research at the largest library in the world?"

I smile. "That's easy! Greece. Metalworking. I want to talk with that boy." I scan the circular room and find a wooden podium with a sign that says "Reference Assistant." I walk over to it and wait.

"Hello, Arcade." It shouldn't be a surprise to me that

she's the one to arrive at the podium, but it is. That's how Ruah rolls.

"Ruah. You're young again!"

The glow from the three Ts on her ball cap shine out and reflect off the gold walls in the reading room. "Your adventures are reviving me, Arcade. And now that you have that token for good, I think this is how I'll stay."

"There's one more thing, Ruah. I want to talk to the boy."

"Boy?"

"Yes. Theo Timon Theros. Triple T. That's what the Ts stand for, right?"

"Well, yes. That's one way to look at it. There's also Travel, Testing, and—"

"Truth! Yes, I know that now. Get truth and never sell it. Lenwood Badger offered me money for the token, but I didn't sell it. Kenwood tried to get him to see clearly, but he refused."

Ruah frowns. "Yes. Gertrude will be sad about that."

"Gertrude? You *know* her?"

Ruah nods. "We had a little token exchange. After your birth. We both knew the token needed to be protected, so I kept it safe until you were older and in a different town, away from her grandsons."

Whoa! So much truth. But I need more.

"Ruah, where's the boy? The maker of the mold?"

Ruah smiles. "You'll have to look him up."

"Of course! I got this! Let's see . . . what's the Dewey number for Metalworking?"

Ruah shakes her head. "It's not like that here. Too many volumes. They use a different system."

"They do?" I turn to my sister. "A different way of thinking? Right here in the largest library in the world? Imagine that!" I poke her in the ribs.

Zoe smirks. "So how you gonna find it, Einstein? You know Dewey, but—"

"The volumes are categorized using the alphabet," Ruah says. "So where would you like to start?"

Zoe laughs. "Okay. M, right?"

"Absolutely not." I turn and point to Ruah's hat. "I'd like to go to the Ts, please."

She nods. "Great choice."

We follow Ruah under one of the archways in the circular reading room. "Ts will be down here."

"But I don't get it!" Zoe says. "How does a T relate to metalworking?"

"Trust, Zoe!" I laugh. "That's a T too!"

She rolls her eyes.

I gasp when I see the sign. "TECHNOLOGY. Wow." I run my fingers over the spines on the books until I get to the subset TT. "Handicrafts, Arts and Crafts." Then I bend down to look at one of the lower shelves. The numbers come into view.

TT223—METALWORKING

"Ruah! This is CRAZY! Do you how many times the number twenty-three has popped into my life? My elementary school was PS 23, my middle school is 230, I've

been on the twenty-third floor a bunch of times, there was that café, Chill 23, and today is . . . February twenty-third!"

Ruah laughs. "'Get the truth and never sell it.' Proverbs 23:23."

I start to pull a book out from the shelf when a finger taps me on the shoulder. I straighten . . . and I turn . . .

And I come face-to-face with the maker of the Triple T mold.

Theo Timon Theros. And he's holding the Triple T Token.

He smiles. "Hello, Arcade Livingston. I hear we have a lot in common."

I stand there, frozen, staring at this light-skinned boy with curly brown hair that falls into his eyes.

He's been working so hard he hasn't had time for a haircut.

"Theo? Hey, man. How's it goin?" is all I can think to say as I hold out my fist.

He looks at it, gives a puzzled look, and then acts like he remembers something. "Oh, yes, Ruah told me about this." He smiles and he gives me a fist bump. "Hello, Zoe." He holds a fist out to her. "You two have been on some amazing Arcade Adventures. I have loved every minute."

"How do you know where we've been?" I remember the person that Celeste saw on the top of the dome. "Have you been watching?"

He shakes his head. "Not in person. I've been imagining as Ruah tells me the stories."

"She tells you stories? When? Where?"

He smiles. "At the amphitheater in Arcadia, during my lunch breaks from work! She brings the token, and she tells me where you are and what you're doing. When I hear the stories, I feel like I'm there with you, laughing, joking, playing, and learning. It's what I've always wanted to do. Arcade, you are the fulfillment of the wish I made on my twelfth birthday."

"Wait." Zoe holds a hand up. "How *exactly* can that happen? You're from ancient Greece, and we're from, well . . . now, New York City. And it seems so scattered, so random. The elevators go all over the world, and when we get back, no time has passed. How can our adventures line up with your breaks? It doesn't make sense."

I laugh. "Time travel. Who can understand it? But it makes sense to me."

One side of Theo's mouth turns up in a grin, and he holds up the token. "Do you want to go on an adventure together?"

"That would be awesome!" Zoe and I follow Theo to the center of the reading room. There's a golden elevator waiting in the middle, complete with a golden coin slot, and a sign that says GET TRUTH. Theo takes the token and drops it in the slot.

"What's next for Arcade Livingston?" Theo asks. "How do you do that hand thing?"

"What hand thing?"

"The one that opens the doors."

"Oh, that one." I put my palms together and pull them apart.

Theo nods. "Oh, yes. That makes sense. Let's do it together."

We stand side by side and motion the doors to open. When they do, all three of us step in. When we do, they turn to glass.

"Oh, no. This is not good," Zoe says.

"Oh, yes, it is! We can finally see clearly where we're going!"

The doors close, and the elevator rises. Slowly, so we can take in every inch of the golden dome. Statues of great leaders in history guard the dome. And as we go up further, we get to read the plaques!

They're all about wisdom, knowledge, self-discipline, and . . . truth.

There are two that shine out the brightest. As I read them, my voice catches.

"As one lamp lights another, nor grows less, so nobleness enkindleth nobleness."

And the other . . .

"What doth the Lord require of thee, but to do justly, to love mercy, and to walk humbly with thy God?"

Theo smiles. "You are a lamp of nobleness, Arcade. And you have acted justly, mercifully, and humbly with God's help. You are the b-EST person to own the Triple T Token. Do you believe that?"

Zoe puts a hand on my shoulder. "Do you believe it?"

I nod. "I do. It's the truth."

Theo jumps up. "Then let's GOOOOOOOOOO!"

The elevator cranks up speed and shoots upward, freaking me out as we near the top of the dome! There's a picture of a woman up there.

"Don't be alarmed," Theo says, "She represents Human Understanding."

Of course.

A hole opens, and our elevator shoots through the top. We go through what looks like golden flames, but if they're hot, we don't feel them. The elevator stops for a second, and we look down.

"The Torch of Knowledge," Theo says.

"ZOE! MY BOOKENDS HAVE A TORCH ON THE TOP!"

"Huh?"

"The bookends Mom and Dad gave me are a replica of this building! The larg-EST library in the world!"

Zoe gasps. "They always give the perfect gifts."

I suddenly remember something. "Mom's travel journal! ZOE, MOM LEFT A TRAVEL JOURNAL between the bookends! Do you think it's all about her Arcade Adventures with Dad?"

Zoe smiles and puts her hand over her heart. "I guess we have some reading to do when we get home!"

The elevator shoots higher and higher—through the clouds and beyond. Soon we are in space, with stars that seem just beyond our reach, and a beautiful, blue planet below.

"Promise me you'll keep going on adventures, okay, Arcade? As long as there are no limits to your imagination, there will be no limits for me either," says Theo.

"I promise."

And right then, something heavy clunks on my chest. I put my hand on my heart. I know just what it is.

The Golden Travel Guide.

The Fiery Metal Tester.

The Dazzling Truth Detector.

Better known as . . .

The Triple T Token.

And I can only think of one thing to say.

"THAT'S DOOOOOOOOOOOOPE!"

THE END

Arcade and the Dazzling Truth Detector Discussion Questions

1. If you could wish for any experience on your next birthday (and you know it would be granted), what would it be? Why? How could you use that experience to help others? Imagine the possibilities!

2. Which -est would you most like to explore? Highest? Lowest? Widest? Deepest? Longest? Or some other -est? Why did you pick that one? Take a trip to the library (or to your favorite internet research site, with parent or teacher permission) and make a list of all the places, people, and things, that fit into the category of your favorite -est, then find out all you can about them!

3. Do you have a person in your life who challenges you to be a better person? Who is it, and what do they do that specifically challenges you? How can you challenge others in this way?

4. Where do you look to GET TRUTH in your life? Your family, your friends, books, the internet? How might some of these sources mislead you? What is your ultimate source of truth? Arcade's family's ultimate source of truth is God's Word—the Bible. Have you ever looked into that? Why or why not?

5. Do you have a favorite quote about knowledge, wisdom, or truth? What is it? Who said it or wrote it, and why is what they said meaningful to you?

6. What does it mean to you to *do justly, love mercy, and walk humbly*? You might have to look those words up in a dictionary!

7. Do you ask a lot of questions? How do you feel when you can't find an answer to a question? Are you comfortable accepting that some things in life are a mystery? Why or why not?

8. A large portion of Arcade's story takes place in New York City. Have you ever been there? If so, what was your favorite place to visit? If you haven't been, is there a place that you'd like to visit that was described in the Arcade series? Why does that place interest you? (You may want to do some research on that place at the library or online.)

9. Hey you . . . wake up! Mr. Dooley just gave you an assignment to write about time travel. Is it possible? What do you know about science that could lead you to believe in time travel? Convince him! (Make this fun. Use your God-given creativity and imagination.)

10. Arcade has trouble seeing the truth about the token and himself until he gets new glasses from Elena's dad. Do you think the problem was Arcade's eyesight, or was it something else that kept him from seeing the truth he needed to see? What kinds of things blind us from seeing the truth about ourselves and others?

11. Elena tells Arcade that it was no accident that the volleyball hit him in the face. What do you think she meant by that? Do you believe in coincidence, or do you believe everything happens for a purpose? Why do you hold that belief?

12. Arcade, Zoe, Kevin, and Casey—four African-American preteens—find themselves in the presence of President Abraham Lincoln just as he's about to sign the Emancipation Proclamation—a document that changed the course of history for African-Americans. Do you feel a special connection to a particular event in history? Research that, and be amazed!

13. The number 23 shows up in all four Arcade books in different ways. (Twenty-three is my favorite number.) Can you

remember all the references to the number 23? Do you have a recurring number or word in your life? If so, does it hold a special significance for you and if so, what is that significance? Again—imagine the possibilities!

14. Arcade tells Elena, "-Ests just don't happen by accident." Think about the bravest, toughest, brightest, funniest, happiest people you know. Do you believe that God created them that way for a purpose? Do you know that you are God's b-est? Research that! It's the truth!

15. So now you know what the Ts on the Triple T Token stand for: Travel, Testing, and Truth. How have these three Ts affected your life? Have you traveled? What kinds of tests have you been through (not just school tests)? What truths have you learned about yourself and others? My prayer for you is that you will keep your eyes and your heart open to life's adventures, and that you will use what you learn in every one to help others be their best selves!

Acknowledgments

Thank you, Lord, for blessing me with the abilities and the guidance to live a life that allows me to accomplish so many things I can't take total credit for. As always, it all starts with you. You give me the desire and the ability to do what pleases you. I pray this series of books makes you proud.

Momma Jennings—Even as you face the sad but joyous loss (and heaven's gain) of Dad and the love of your life, you continue to impress me with your incredible strength! I know we will see Daddy again, but until then, I'll continue to look to you for the unconditional love and unwavering encouragement you have never failed to give. You inspire me to keep striving to be the best man I can be. I'll always strive in all that I do to be there for you and to make you proud!

Jill Osborne, Keith Bell, Zondervan/ Zonderkidz—We are about to publish my fifth book! I'm stunned! I just want to thank you all for your hard work in helping me make The Coin Slot Chronicles a reality! I hope that we can keep this adventure going, but to have come this far after being a kid who suffered from a reading deficit, is something I could never have imagined nor ever hoped to accomplish without your help and motivation!

Every kid who reads Arcade's Coin Slot Chronicles—If there were no you, there would be no #ShadTheKidsAuthor. I hope that, thus far, I have inspired you to face life with positivity and hope, to go for your dreams, to take personal responsibility, to make no excuses, to work hard, to keep the faith, and to always . . . always . . . ENJOY THE RIDE!

Check out these other books in the Coin Slot Chronicles series:

Arcade and the Fiery Metal Tester